CHILDREN'S CLASSICS
EVERYMAN'S LIBRARY

Nursery Rhymes

Walter Jerrold

Mother Goose's Nursery Rhymes

*With Illustrations
by Charles Robinson*

EVERYMAN'S LIBRARY
CHILDREN'S CLASSICS
Alfred A. Knopf New York London Toronto

THIS IS A BORZOI BOOK
PUBLISHED BY ALFRED A. KNOPF

First published 1903 by Blackie & Son, Ltd., London,
as *The Big Book of Nursery Rhymes*
First included in Everyman's Library Children's Classics 1993
Book design by Barbara de Wilde, Carol Devine Carson
and Peter B. Willberg

Second printing (US)

Five of Ernest H. Shepard's illustrations from *Dream Days* by
Kenneth Grahame are reprinted on the endpapers by permission of
The Bodley Head, London. The sixth illustration is by S. C. Hulme Beaman.

All rights reserved under International and Pan-American Copyright Conventions.
Published in the United States by Alfred A. Knopf, a division of Random House,
Inc., New York, and simultaneously in Canada by Random House of Canada
Limited, Toronto. Distributed by Random House, Inc., New York.
Published in the United Kingdom by Everyman's Library, Gloucester Mansions,
140A Shaftesbury Avenue, London WC2H 8HD. Distributed by
Random House (UK) Ltd.

www.randomhouse.com/everymans

ISBN 0-679-42815-1 (US)
1-85715-921-7 (UK)

A CIP catalogue record for this book is available from the British Library
Library of Congress Cataloging-in-Publication Data
Mother Goose.
[Big book of nursery rhymes]
Mother Goose's nursery rhymes / edited by Walter Jerrold.
p.   cm.—(Everyman's library children's classics)
Previously published as: The Big book of nursery rhymes.
Includes bibliographical references.
Summary: A collection of traditional rhymes.
ISBN 0-679-42815-1
1. Nursery rhymes.   2. Children's poetry. [1. Nursery rhymes.]
I. Title.   II. Series

PZ8.3.M85   1993   93-22604
398.8—dc20   CIP
                                                              AC

Printed and bound in Germany by GGP Media, Pössneck

DEDICATION

To the Youngest
Baby of All with
the Love of the
Compiler and the
Artist. Xmas 1903.

INTRODUCTION.

THE very title "Nursery Rhymes", which has come to be associated with a great body of familiar verse, is in itself sufficient evidence of how that verse has been passed down from generation to generation. Some pieces date, perhaps, from hundreds of years ago, and had been repeated thousands of times before they were printed. There are not wanting learned folk who tell us that there was once, in Britain, a King Cole, and that the only relic of his reign which we have is the verse in which he is shown calling for his pipe, his bowl, and his fiddlers three. Such wise people forget that pipes were not smoked here before the days of Queen Elizabeth, and that fiddles were not known before the sixteenth century. It is certain, however, that some of these rhymes were familiar in those great days; Shakespeare seems to refer to one

6

of them, and some of his fellow-dramatists refer to others. But to trace them all back to their original appearances would need a long life spent in patient investigation, and on tracing each verse to its first appearance in print we should be no nearer to the ascertaining of the authorship of the majority of these most popular of all popular poems. It is but of a few items that we can name the authorship. "A Frog he would a - wooing Go" was composed by Liston, the comedian who won fame by his impersonation of the inquisitive Paul Pry, but Liston based on an early series of verses on a similar theme, which the curious in such matters may find without much difficulty. "Wee Willie Winkie" was written by the nineteenth-century Scots poet, William Miller, and soon became traditional, taking its place with time-honoured companions. "There was an old Woman tossed up in a Basket" (or blanket, for there are, as usual, differing versions) it has been suggested may have been written by Oliver Goldsmith, whose "Elegy on a Mad Dog" has by some compilers been included in Nursery Rhymes, and who is also credited with the invention of that dear little nursery companion Goody Two-Shoes.

Since the first collection of Nursery Rhymes was published, rather more than one hundred and forty years ago, there have been almost countless issues, of an ever-increasing size as fresh traditional material has been collected, yet the oral origin

of the rhymes is shown by the many variants existing. I have listened to different persons repeating such simple lines as "This Little Pig went to Market", "Hush-a-bye Baby on the Tree Top", and other of the most familiar of the verses, and have found that in each family where I have heard them there have been some slight verbal differences between them and the forms in which I recall them, either from recollections of childhood or from subsequent reading. A variorum edition of our Nursery Rhymes would indeed run into many volumes; each piece might almost be made the subject of a separate treatise were anyone disposed to undertake the thankless task. Indeed, the Rhymes have been more badly used even than that, for a writer, some sixty years ago, sought to show that none of them meant what they appeared to mean, but were all of them mere medleys of words consequent upon the writing down of deeply significant Dutch phrases in phonetic fashion. Truly what the nursery would describe as "double Dutch"!

Tradition in the nursery has acted as a severe editor. In many instances lengthy rhymes, or rhymes which were lengthy when they left their authors' hands, have been rigorously cut down to a few lines. Thus has it been with the ballad of "Jack Horner", his giant-killing exploits are forgotten, and all that we now delight in recalling is that he extracted a plum from a Christmas-pie and was smugly self-satisfied thereat; of the chapbook tale in verse recounting the strange adventures of Jack and Jill (or Gill, as it used to be), but one or two stanzas are now generally current—most people remember but one; "One Misty Moisty Morning" is the first stanza out of fifteen forming an old song known as "The Wiltshire Wedding".

The earliest known collection of Nursery Rhymes was published about 1760 by John Newbery, the first publisher who made it his business to cater for little readers. That collection formed a tiny book containing two or three dozen short pieces supplemented by the songs from Shakespeare's plays. Some strange titles were given to the rhymes: "Ding, Dong, Bell" was known as "Plato's Song", while "There were two Birds sat on a Stone" was "Aristotle's Song"; then, too, to each rhyme was appended a moral maxim, as, for example, to "Is John Smith within?" is added "Knowledge is a treasure, but practice is the key to it". Most of the rhymes in this little Newbery collection: "There was a little Man and he wooed a little Maid", "The Wise Men of Gotham", &c., are repeated in the present volume so far as may be in accordance with that early text. Others have been compared with such early issues as I have been able to find in old chap-books issued late in the eighteenth century or early in the nineteenth. With the last century the rhymes became the subject of scholarly research, though Joseph Ritson had issued

his *Gammer Gurton's Garland* as early as 1781;
James Orchard Halliwell (afterwards Halliwell-
Phillipps), sixty years later, made a considerable
collection, and on their volumes subsequent ones
have necessarily very largely been based. Students
divide our rhymes into narrative pieces, historical,
folk-lore, game rhymes, counting-out rhymes, jingles,
fragments, &c., but for the children for whom and
by whom they are remembered, and for whom they
are here collected and pictured anew, they are just
Nursery Rhymes.

WALTER JERROLD

CONTENTS

Contents

Contents

Contents

Contents

Contents

Contents

B

Contents

Contents

"Herebe !
ginsthe !!
bigbo !!!
okofnur!!!!
se!ryrh! ymes !

THE ♥ ♥
QUEEN *of*
HEARTS

The Queen of Hearts she
made some tarts,

All on a summer's day;

The Knave of Hearts he stole those
tarts,

And took them clean away.

The Queen of Hearts

The King of Hearts
called for those
tarts,

And beat the
Knave full
sore.

The Knave of Hearts

    brought back those tarts,

And vowed he 'd steal no more.

SAINT SWITHIN'S DAY

St. Swithin's day, if thou dost rain,
For forty days it will remain;
St. Swithin's day, if thou be fair,
For forty days 't will rain no more.

DANCE TO YOUR DADDIE

Dance to your daddie,
My bonnie laddie,
Dance to your daddie, my bonnie lamb!
You shall get a fishie
On a little dishie,
You shall get a fishie when the boat comes hame!

Dance to your daddie,
My bonnie laddie,
Dance to your daddie, and to your mammie sing!
You shall get a coatie,
And a pair of breekies,
You shall get a coatie when the boat comes in!

THE MAN IN THE MOON

The man in the
   moon
Came tumbling
   down
And asked the way
   to Norwich;
He went by the
   south,
And burnt his
   mouth
With eating cold
   pease porridge.

28

Simple Simon

SIMPLE SIMON

SIMPLE SIMON met a pie-man,
    Going to the fair;
Says Simple Simon to the pie-man,
    " Let me taste your ware."

Says the pie-man unto Simon,
    " First give me a penny."
Says Simple Simon to the pie-man,
    " I have not got any."

He went to catch a dicky-bird,
    And thought he could not fail,
Because he had got a little salt
    To put upon his tail.

Simple Simon

He went to
ride a
spotted cow,

That had got
a little
calf,

She threw him
down upon
the ground,

Which made
the people
laugh.

Simple Simon

Then Simple Simon went a-hunting,
    For to catch a hare,
He rode a goat about the street,
    But could not find one there.

He went for to eat honey
    Out of the mustard-pot,
He bit his tongue until he cried,
    That was all the good he got.

Simple Simon

SIMPLE SIMON went a-fishing
    For to catch a whale;
And all the water he had got
    Was in his mother's pail.

He went to take a bird's nest,
    Was built upon a bough;
A branch gave way, and Simon fell
    Into a dirty slough.

He went to shoot a
    wild duck,
    But the wild duck
      flew away;
Says Simon, " I can't
    hit him,
    Because he will not
      stay."

Simple Simon

NCE Simon made a great
    Snowball,
  And brought it in to roast;
  He laid it down before the
    fire,
  And soon the ball was lost.

HE went to slide upon the ice,
  Before the ice would bear;
  Then he plunged in above his
    knees,
  Which made poor Simon stare.

He went to try if cherries ripe
  Grew upon a thistle;
He pricked his finger very much,
  Which made poor Simon whistle.

He washed himself with blacking-ball,
　Because he had no soap:
Then, then, said to his mother,
　" I 'm a beauty now, I hope."

He went for water in a sieve,
　But soon it all ran through;
And now poor Simple Simon
　Bids you all adieu.

TOAD AND FROG

" Croak," said the toad, " I 'm hungry
    I think,
To-day I 've had nothing to eat or
    to drink;
I 'll crawl to a garden and jump
    through the pales,
And there I 'll dine nicely on slugs and on snails."

" Ho, ho!" quoth the frog, " is that what you mean?
Then I 'll hop away to the next meadow stream,
There I will drink, and eat worms and slugs too,
And then I shall have a good dinner like you."

LITTLE
JACK HORNER

Little Jack Horner
    Sat in a corner
Eating of Christmas pie;

He put in his thumb,
    And pulled out a plum,
And cried " What a good boy
    was I!"

THE WOOING

There was a little man,
Who wooed a little maid;
And he said: "Little maid, will you wed, wed, wed?
I have little more to say,
So will you ay or nay
For the least said is soonest mend-ed, ded, ded."

Then the little maid replied:
"Should I be your little bride,
Pray what must we have for to eat, eat, eat?
Will the flame that you're so rich in
Light a fire in the kitchen?
Or the little god of Love turn the spit, spit, spit?"

HANDY PANDY

Handy Pandy,

   Jack-a-Dandy,

Loves plum-cake

   and sugar-candy;

He bought some

   at a grocer's shop,

     And out he came, hop, hop, hop,

The Kilkenny Cats

There were once two cats of Kilkenny,

Each thought there was one cat too many;

So they fought and they fit,

And they scratched and they bit,

Till, excepting their nails

And the tips of their tails,

Instead of two cats, there weren't any.

BLOW·WIND·BLOW·

Blow, wind, blow! and go, mill, go!

That the miller may grind his corn;

That the baker may take it, and into rolls make it,

And send us some hot in the morn.

ONE, TWO, THREE, AND FOUR LEGS

Two legs sat upon three legs,
With one leg in his lap;
In comes four legs,
And runs away with one leg.

Up jumps two legs,
Catches up three legs,
Throws it after four legs,
And makes him bring back one leg.

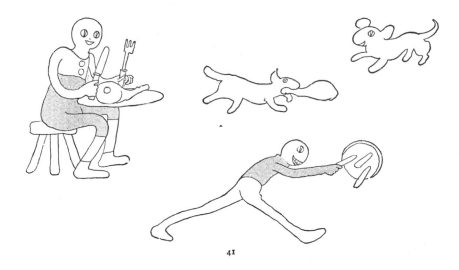

BLUE BELL BOY

I HAD a little boy,
    And called him Blue Bell;
Gave him a little work,
    He did it very well.

I bade him go upstairs
    To bring me a gold pin;
In coal-scuttle fell he,
Up to his little chin.

He went to the garden
    To pick a little sage;
He tumbled on his nose,
    And fell into a rage.

He went to the cellar
    To draw a little beer;
And quickly did return
    To say there was none there.

Cock-a-doodle-do

COCK-A-DOODLE-DO

Cock-a-doodle-do!
My dame has lost her shoe;
My master's lost his fiddle-stick,
And don't know what to do.

Cock-a-doodle-do!
What is my dame to do?
Till master finds his fiddle-stick,
She'll dance without her shoe.

JOHN COOK'S GREY MARE

JOHN COOK had a little grey mare; he, haw, hum!
Her back stood up, and her bones they were bare; he, haw, hum!

John Cook was riding up Shuter's bank; he, haw, hum!
And there his nag did kick and prank; he, haw, hum!

John Cook was riding up Shuter's hill; he, haw, hum!
His mare fell down, and she made her will; he, haw, hum!

The bridle and saddle were laid on the shelf; he, haw, hum!
If you want any more you may sing it yourself; he, haw, hum!

45

BUZ AND HUM

B UZ, quoth the blue
fly,
Hum, quoth the
bee,
Buz and hum they
cry,
And so do we.

In his ear, in his nose,
Thus, do you see?
He ate the dormouse,
Else it was he.

TOMMY
TITTLEMOUSE

Little Tommy Tittlemouse
Lived in a little house;
He caught fishes
In other men's ditches.

46

A AND B AND SEE

Great A, little a, bounc-
    ing B,

The cat's in the cup-
    board and she can't
    see.

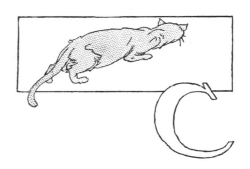

DOCTOR FOSTER

OCTOR Foster went
    to Glo'ster,

In a shower of
    rain;

He stepped in a puddle right up to his middle,

And never went there again.

47

DAFFY·DOWN·DILLY·

Daffy-down-dilly has come to town,

In a yellow petticoat, and a green
   gown.

48

HO MY KITTEN

HO my kitten, a kitten,
    And ho! my kitten, my deary!
Such a sweet pet as this
    Was neither far nor neary.

Here we go up, up, up,
    Here we go down, down, down;
Here we go backwards and forwards,
    And here we go round, round, round.

LAVENDER BLUE

LAVENDER blue and rosemary green,
When I am king you shall be queen;
Call up my maids at four o'clock,
Some to the wheel and some to the
    rock,
Some to make hay and some to shear
    corn,
And you and I will keep ourselves warm.

49   D

The QUARREL SOME KITTENS

TWO little kittens one stormy
    night,
They began to quarrel and
    they began to fight;
One had a mouse and the
    other had none,
And that's the way the quarrel begun.

"I'll have that mouse," said the biggest cat.
"You'll have that mouse? we'll see about that!"
"I will have that mouse," said the eldest son.
"You sha'n't have the mouse," said the little one.

I told you before 't was a stormy night
When these two little kittens began to fight;
The old woman seized her sweeping broom,
And swept the two kittens right out of the room.

The Quarrelsome Kittens

The ground was covered with frost and snow,
And the two little kittens had nowhere to go;
So they laid them down on the mat at the door,
While the old woman finished sweeping the floor.

Then they crept in, as quiet as mice,
All wet with the snow, and as cold as ice,
For they found it was better, that stormy night,
To lie down and sleep than to quarrel and fight.

THE FLY AND THE HUMBLE-BEE

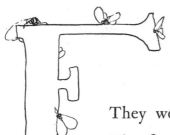

IDDLE-DE-DEE, fiddle-de-dee,
   The fly shall marry the humble-
      bee;

They went to church and married was she,
The fly has married the humble-bee.

CAT AND DOG

Pussy sits beside the fire,
   How can she be fair?
In comes the little dog,
   " Pussy, are you
      there?

So, so, Mistress Pussy,
   Pray, how do you
      do?"
" Thank you, thank
   you, little dog,
I 'm very well just
   now."

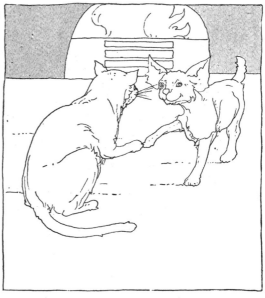

BOBBY SHAFT

Bobby Shaft is gone to sea,
With silver buckles at his knee;
When he'll come home he'll marry me,
Pretty Bobby Shaft!

Bobby Shaft is fat and fair,
Combing down his yellow hair;
He's my love for evermore!
Pretty Bobby Shaft!

THE LITTLE CLOCK

There 's a neat little clock,
   In the schoolroom it stands,
And it points to the time
   With its two little hands.
And may we, like the clock,
Keep a face clean and bright,
With hands ever ready
To do what is right.

LITTLE MAID

"Little maid, pretty maid,
   whither goest thou?"
"Down in the forest to milk
   my cow."
"Shall I go with thee?" "No,
   not now;
When I send for thee, then
   come thou."

BAT.
BAT,

Bat, bat,
  Come under my hat,
And I 'll give you a slice
    of bacon;

And when I bake,
  I 'll give you a cake,
If I am not mistaken.

CHRISTMAS

Christmas is coming, the geese are
getting fat,

Please to put a penny in an old
man's hat;

If you have n't got a penny, a ha'-
penny will do,

If you have n't got a ha'penny, God
bless you.

PETER WHITE

Peter White will ne'er go
right,

And would you know the
reason why?

He follows his nose where'er
he goes,

And that stands all awry.

SLEEP·BABY·SLEEP·

LEEP, baby, sleep,
Our cottage vale is
    deep;
The little lamb is on the green,
With woolly fleece so soft
  and clean—
    Sleep, baby, sleep!

Sleep, baby, sleep,
Down where the wood-
    bines creep;
Be always like the lamb so mild,
A kind, and sweet, and gentle
  child—
    Sleep, baby, sleep!

UP PIPPEN HILL

As I was going up Pippen
     Hill,
  Pippen Hill was dirty;
There I met a pretty miss,
  And she dropped me a
       curtsey.

Little miss, pretty miss,
  Blessings light upon you!
If I had half a crown a day,
  I'd spend it all upon you.

A FALLING OUT

LITTLE old man and I
     fell out;
  How shall we bring
     this matter about?
Bring it about as
     well as you can;
Get you gone, you
     little old man.

Tom, Tom, the Piper's Son

TOM, THE PIPER'S SON

Tom, Tom, the piper's son,
Stole a pig and away he run!
The pig was eat and Tom was beat,
And Tom went howling down the street.

PEG

Peg, Peg, with a wooden leg,
  Her father was a miller;
He tossed the dumpling at
    her head,
  And said he could not
    kill her.

A DIFFICULT RHYME

What is the rhyme for
  porringer?
The king he had a
  daughter fair,
And gave the Prince
  of Orange her.

THE OLD WOMAN TOSSED IN A BASKET

There was an old woman tossed up in a basket

Seventeen times as high as the moon;

Where she was going I couldn't but ask it,

For in her hand she carried a broom.

"Old woman, old woman, old woman," quoth I,

"Where are you going to up so high?"

"To brush the cobwebs off the sky!"

"May I go with thee?" "Aye, by-and-by."

62

POOR OLD ROBINSON CRUSOE

OOR old Robinson Crusoe!
Poor old Robinson Crusoe!
They made him a coat
Of an old nanny goat,
   I wonder why they could
     do so!
With a ring a ting tang,
And a ring a ting tang,
Poor old Robinson Crusoe!

TWO LITTLE DOGS

Two little dogs sat by the fire,
  Over a fender of coal-dust;
When one said to the other dog,
   "If Pompey won't talk, why,
    I must."

SATURDAY. SUNDAY

On Saturday night
    Shall be all my care
To powder my locks
    And curl my hair.

On Sunday morning
    My love will come in,
When he will marry me
    With a gold ring.

THE OWL IN THE OAK

THERE was an owl lived in an oak,

Whiskey, whaskey, weedle;

And all the words he ever spoke

Were fiddle, faddle, feedle.

A sportsman chanced to come that way,

Whiskey, whaskey, weedle;

Says he, "I'll shoot you, silly bird,

So fiddle, faddle, feedle!"

GEORGY PORGY

Georgy Porgy, pudding and pie,

Kissed the girls and made them cry.

When the boys came out to play,

Georgy Porgy ran away.

E

TO MARKET

To market, to market,
 To buy a fat pig;
Home again, home again,
 Jiggety jig.

To market, to market,
 To buy a fat hog;
Home again, home again,
 Jiggety jog.

66

THE LITTLE GUINEA-PIG

There was a little Guinea-Pig,
Who, being little, was not big;
He always walked upon his feet,
And never fasted when he eat.

When from a place he ran away,
He never at that place did stay;
And while he ran, as I am told,
He ne'er stood still for young or old.

He often squeak'd and sometimes vi'lent,
And when he squeak'd he ne'er was silent:
Though ne'er instructed by a cat,
He knew a mouse was not a rat.

One day, as I am certified,
He took a whim, and fairly died;
And, as I 'm told by men of sense,
He never has been living since.

A
NICK AND A NOCK

A nick and a nock,
A hen and a cock,
And a penny for my master.

PANCAKE DAY

Great A, little A,
This is pancake day;
Toss the ball high,
Throw the ball low,
Those that come after
May sing heigh-ho!

HUSH·A· BYE·BABY

HUSH-
a-bye,
baby,

On the
tree top,

When the
wind blows,

The cradle
will rock;

When the bough breaks,
The cradle will fall,

Down tumbles baby,
Cradle, and all.

IN MARBLE HALLS

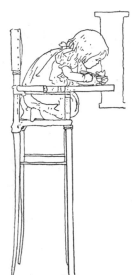

IN marble halls as white as milk,
    Lined with a skin as soft as silk;

Within a fountain crystal clear,
A golden apple doth appear;

No doors there are to this strong-
    hold,
Yet thieves break in and steal the
    gold.

JACK SPRAT'S PIG

Jack Sprat had a pig, who was not very little,
    Nor yet very big;

He was not very lean, he was not very fat;

He'll do well for a grunt,
Says little Jack Sprat.

ROBIN-A-BOBIN

Robin-a-Bobin
Bent his bow,
Shot at a pigeon,
And killed a crow.

BANDY-LEGS

As I was going to sell
my eggs,
I met a man with bandy
legs;
Bandy legs and crooked
toes,
I tripped up his heels,
and he fell on his
nose.

71

A APPLE
PIE

A was an apple pie

B bit it.

C cut it,

D dealt it;

E eat it,

F fought for it,

G got it,

H had it,

J joined it;

K kept it,

L longed for it,

M mourned for it,

N nodded for it,

O opened it,

P peeped in it,

Q quartered it,

R ran for it,

S stole it,

T took it,

V viewed it,

W wanted it,

X Y Z and all wished a piece of it

THE
PUMPKIN EATER

Peter, Peter, pumpkin eater,

Had a wife and could n't keep
her;

He put her in a pumpkin shell,

And there he kept her very
well.

HUSH-A-BYE, BABY

Hush-a-bye, baby,
Daddy is near;
Mamma is a lady,
And that 's very clear.

BIRDS OF A FEATHER

BIRDS of a feather flock
together,

And so will pigs and
swine;

Rats and mice will have
their choice,

And so will I have
mine.

COCK-A-DOODLE-DO

Oh, my pretty cock! Oh, my hand-
some cock!

I pray you, do not crow before
day,

And your comb shall be made of
the very beaten gold,

And your wings of the silver so
gray.

76

HUSH, BABY, MY DOLLY

Hush, baby, my dolly, I pray you don't cry,

And I'll give you some bread and some milk
by and by;

Or perhaps you like custard, or maybe a tart,

Then to either you're welcome, with all my
heart.

I HAD A LITTLE PONY

I HAD a little pony
His name was Dapple-Grey,
I lent him to a lady,
To ride a mile away.
She whipped him, she lashed him,
She rode him through the mire;
I would not lend my pony now
For all the lady's hire.

SNAIL

Snail, snail, come out of
your hole,
Or else I'll beat you as
black as a coal.
Snail, snail, put out your
horns,
Here comes a thief to pull
down your walls.

73

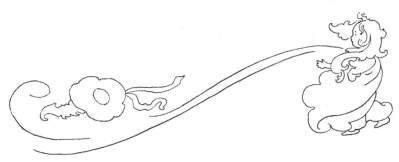

MY LADY WIND

My lady Wind, my lady Wind,
Went round about the house to find
   A chink to get her foot in:
She tried the keyhole in the door,
She tried the crevice in the floor,
   And drove the chimney soot in.

And then one night, when it was dark,
She blew up such a tiny spark,
   That all the house was pothered:
From it she raised up such a flame,
As flamed away to Belting Lane,
   And White Cross folks were smothered.

And thus when once, my little dears,
A whisper reaches itching ears,
   The same will come, you'll find:
Take my advice, restrain the tongue,
Remember what old nurse has sung
   Of busy lady Wind!

LITTLE JENNY WREN

A S little Jenny Wren
      Was sitting by the shed,
She waggled with her tail,
      And nodded with her head.

She waggled with her tail,
      And nodded with her head,
As little Jenny Wren
      Was sitting by the shed.

POOR ROBIN

The north wind doth blow,
And we shall have snow,
And what will poor Robin do
    then?
      Poor thing!

He'll sit in a barn,
And to keep himself warm
Will hide his head under his
    wing.
      Poor thing!

DANCE, LITTLE BABY

Dance, little Baby, dance up high,
Never mind, Baby, Mother is by;
Crow and caper, caper and crow,
There, little Baby, there you go;
Up to the ceiling, down to the
  ground,
Backwards and forwards, round
  and round;
Dance, little Baby, and Mother
  will sing,
With the merry coral, ding, ding, ding!

OF WASHING

They that wash on Friday, wash
  in need;

And they that wash on Saturday,
  oh! they 're sluts indeed.

DICKERY, DICKERY, DARE

Dickery,
dickery,
dare,

The
pig
flew
up
in
the
air;

The
man
in
brown
soon
brought
him
down,

Dickery,
dickery,
dare.

THE HOUSE THAT JACK BUILT

This is the house that Jack built.

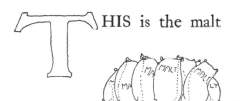

THIS is the malt

That lay in the house that Jack built.

This is the rat,

That ate the malt
That lay in the house that Jack built.

The House that Jack Built

This is the cat,
That killed the rat,
That ate the malt
That lay in the house that Jack built.

This is the dog,
That worried the cat,
That killed the rat,
That ate the malt
That lay in the house that Jack built.

This is the cow with the crum-
    pled horn,
That tossed the dog,
That worried the cat,
That killed the rat,
That ate the malt
That lay in the house that Jack built.

This is the maiden all forlorn,
That milked the cow with the crum-
    pled horn,
That tossed the dog,
That worried the cat,
That killed the rat,
That ate the malt
That lay in the house that Jack built.

The House that Jack Built

This is the man all tattered and
    torn,
That kissed the maiden all forlorn,
That milked the cow with the
    crumpled horn,
That tossed the dog,
That worried the cat,
That killed the rat,
That ate the malt
That lay in the house that Jack
    built.

This is the priest all shaven and shorn,
That married the man all tattered and
    torn,
That kissed the maiden all forlorn,
That milked the cow with the crumpled
    horn,
That tossed the dog,
That worried the cat,
That killed the rat,
That ate the malt
That lay in the house that Jack built.

The House that Jack Built

This is the cock that crowed in the morn,

That waked the priest all shaven and shorn,

That married the man all tattered and torn,

That kissed the maiden all forlorn,

That milked the cow with the crumpled horn,

That tossed the dog,

That worried the cat,

That killed the rat,

That ate the malt

That lay in the house that Jack built.

The House that Jack Built

This is the farmer   sowing his corn,
That kept the cock that   crowed in the morn,
That waked the priest   all shaven and shorn,
    That married the man all tattered and torn,
    That kissed the maiden all forlorn,
    That milked the cow with the crumpled horn,
    That tossed the dog,
    That worried the cat,
    That killed the rat,
    That ate the malt
    That lay in the house that Jack built.

THE MOUSE AND THE MILLER

There was an old woman
Lived under a hill,
She put a mouse in a bag,
And sent it to mill;
The miller did swear
By the point of his knife,
He never took toll
Of a mouse in his life!

LITTLE BETTY BLUE

Little Betty Blue
Lost her holiday shoe,
What shall little Betty
　　do?
Buy her another
To match the other,
And then she 'll walk
　　upon two.

OF THE CUTTING OF NAILS

CUT them on Monday, you cut them for health;

Cut them on Tuesday, you cut them for wealth;

Cut them on Wednesday, you cut them for news;

Cut them on Thursday, a pair of new shoes;

Cut them on Friday, you cut them for sorrow;

Cut them on Saturday, you 'll see your true-love to-morrow;

Cut them on Sunday, and you will have ill fortune all through the week.

THE ORANGE STEALER

Dingty, diddledy, my mammy's maid,

She stole oranges, I 'm afraid;

Some in her pockets, some in her sleeve,

She stole oranges, I do believe.

A FROG HE WOULD A-WOOING GO

A frog he would a-wooing go,
      Heigho! says Rowley,
Whether his mother would let him or no.
    With a rowley powley, gammon and spinach,
    Heigho! says Anthony Rowley.

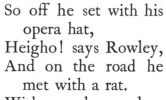

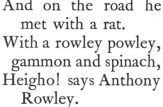

So off he set with his
  opera hat,
Heigho! says Rowley,
And on the road he
  met with a rat.
With a rowley powley,
  gammon and spinach,
Heigho! says Anthony
  Rowley.

"Pray, Mr. Rat, will
  you go with me?"
Heigho! says Rowley,
"Kind Mistress Mous-
  ey for to see!"
With a rowley powley,
  gammon and spinach,
Heigho! says Anthony
  Rowley.

When they reached the
  door of Mousey's hall,
Heigho! says Rowley,
They gave a loud knock,
  and they gave a loud
  call.
With a rowley powley,
  gammon and spinach,
Heigho! says Anthony
  Rowley.

A Frog he would a-wooing go

" Pray, Mistress Mouse, are
  you within?"
    Heigho! says Rowley;
" Oh, yes, kind sirs, I 'm sit-
  ting to spin."
    With a rowley powley,
        gammon and spinach,
Heigho! says Anthony Rowley.

" Pray, Mistress Mouse, will
  you give us some beer?"
    Heigho! says Rowley,
" For Froggy and I are fond
  of good cheer."
    With a rowley powley,
        gammon and spinach,
Heigho! says Anthony Rowley.

" Pray, Mr. Frog, will you
  give us a song?"
    Heigho! says Rowley;
" But let it be something that 's
  not very long."
    With a rowley powley,
        gammon and spinach,
Heigho! says Anthony Rowley.

" Indeed, Mistress Mouse,"
  replied Mr. Frog,
    Heigho! says Rowley,
" A cold has made me as
  hoarse as a hog."
    With a rowley powley,
        gammon and spinach,
Heigho! says Anthony Rowley.

A Frog he would a-wooing go

"Since you have caught cold, Mr. Frog," Mousey said,
    Heigho! says Rowley,
"I 'll sing you a song that I
    have just made."
    With a rowley powley,
        gammon and spinach,
Heigho! says Anthony Rowley.

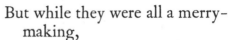

But while they were all a merry-
    making,
    Heigho! says Rowley,
A cat with her kittens came
    tumbling in.
    With a rowley powley,
        gammon and spinach,
Heigho! says Anthony Rowley.

The cat she seized
    the rat by the crown,
    Heigho! says Rowley,
The kittens they pulled
    the little mouse down.
    With a rowley powley, gam
    mon and spinach,
Heigho! says Anthony Rowley.

A Frog he would a-wooing go

This put Mr. Frog in a
  terrible fright,
    Heigho! says Rowley;
He took up his hat and he
  wished them good-night.
    With a rowley powley,
      gammon and spinach,
Heigho! says Anthony Rowley.

But as Froggy was crossing
  over a brook,
    Heigho! says Rowley,
A lily-white duck came and
  gobbled him up.
    With a rowley powley,
      gammon and spinach,
Heigho! says Anthony Rowley.

So there was an end of one, two, and three,
    Heigho! says Rowley,
The Rat, the Mouse, and the little Frog-gee!
    With a rowley powley, gammon and spinach,
    Heigho! says Anthony Rowley.

I LOVE SIXPENCE

I LOVE sixpence, a jolly, jolly sixpence,
I love sixpence as my life;
I spent a penny of it, I spent a penny of it,
I took a penny home to my wife.

I love fourpence, a jolly, jolly fourpence,
I love fourpence as my life;
I spent two pence of it, I spent two pence of it,
And I took two pence home to my wife.

I love nothing, a jolly, jolly nothing,
I love nothing as my life;
I spent nothing of it, I spent nothing of it,
I took nothing home to my wife.

DIDDLEY-DIDDLEY-DUMPTY

IDDLEY-DIDDLEY-DUMPTY,
The cat ran up the plum-tree,
Half a crown
To fetch her down,
Diddley-diddley-dumpty.

SAMMY SOAPSUDS

When little Sammy Soapsuds
Went out to take a ride,
In looking over London Bridge,
He fell into the tide.

His parents never having taught
Their loving Sam to swim,
The tide soon got the mastery,
And made an end of him.

THE WIND

When the wind is in the East,
'T is neither good for man nor beast;
When the wind is in the North,
The skilful fisher goes not forth;
When the wind is in the South,
It blows the bait in the fish's mouth;
When the wind is in the West,
Then 't is at the very best.

A WARNING

THE robin and
the red-breast,
The robin and
the wren;
If ye take from
their nest,
Ye 'll never
thrive again!

The robin and the red-breast,
The martin and the swallow;
If ye touch one of their eggs,
Bad luck will surely follow.

FINGERS AND TOES

Every lady in this land
Has twenty nails upon each hand
Five and twenty on hands and
feet.
All this is true, without deceit.

COCKS crow in the morn
    To tell us to rise,
And he who lies late
    Will never be wise;

For early to bed
    And early to rise,
Is the way to be healthy
    And wealthy and wise.

MY·MAID·MARY·

My maid Mary she minds the dairy,
   While I go a-hoeing and mowing each morn;
Gaily run the reel and the little spinning-wheel,
   Whilst I am singing and mowing my corn.

ROBIN AND WREN

The Robin and the Wren
Fought about the parritch-pan;
And ere the Robin got a spoon,
The Wren had ate the parritch down.

BUY ME A MILKING-PAIL

UY me a milking-pail,
  Mother, mother."
  " Betsy 's gone a-milking,
  Beautiful daughter."

" Sell my father's feather-bed,
  Mother, mother."
" Where will your father lie,
  Beautiful daughter?"

" Put him in the boys' bed,
  Mother, mother."
" Where will the boys lie,
  Beautiful daughter?"

" Put them in the pigs' stye,
  Mother, mother."
" Where will the pigs lie,
  Beautiful daughter?"

" Put them in the salting-tub,
  Mother, mother.
Put them in the salting-tub,
  Mother, mother."

HUMPTY-DUMPTY

HUMPTY-DUMPTY sat on a wall,
Humpty-Dumpty had a great fall;

Threescore men, and threescore more,
Cannot place Humpty-Dumpty as he
was before.

WHAT ARE LITTLE BOYS MADE OF?

What are little boys made of, made of?
What are little boys made of?
Snips and snails, and puppy-dogs' tails;
That's what little boys are made
of, made of.

What are little girls made of,
made of?
What are little girls made of?
Sugar and spice, and all things nice,
That's what little girls are made
of, made of.

THERE WAS A LITTLE MAN

THERE was a little man, and
    he had a little gun,

    And his bullets they were
        made of lead, lead, lead.

    He shot Johnny Sprig through
        the middle of his wig,

And knocked it right
off his head, head,
head.

HARK, HARK! THE DOGS DO BARK

HARK, hark! the dogs do bark,

Beggars are coming to town;

Some in jags, and some in rags,

And some in velvet gown.

BESSY BELL AND MARY GRAY

Bessy Bell and Mary Gray,

They were two bonny lasses;

They built their house upon the lea,

And covered it with rashes.

Bessy kept the garden gate,

And Mary kept the pantry:

Bessy always had to wait,

While Mary lived in plenty.

104

To the BIRDS

AWAY, birds, away!
Take a little, and leave
a little,
And do not come
again;
For if you do,

I will shoot you through,
And there is an end of
you.

HEY! DIDDLE, DIDDLE

HEY! diddle, diddle,

The cat and the fiddle,

The cow jumped over the moon;

The little dog laughed

To see such craft,

And the dish ran away with the
spoon.

TWO LITTLE BIRDS

There were two blackbirds

Sat upon a hill,

The one named Jack,

The other named Jill.

Fly away, Jack!

Fly away, Jill!

Come again, Jack!

Come again, Jill!

THE LITTLE COCK SPARROW

LITTLE Cock Sparrow sat on a green tree,
And he chirruped, he chirruped, so merry was he;
A little Cock Sparrow sat on a green tree,
And he chirruped, he chirruped, so merry was he.

A naughty boy came with his wee bow and arrow,
Determined to shoot this little Cock Sparrow;
A naughty boy came with his wee bow and arrow,
Determined to shoot this little Cock Sparrow.

" This little Cock Sparrow shall make me a stew,
And his giblets shall make me a little pie too."
" Oh, no!" said the sparrow, " I won't make a stew."
So he flapped his wings and away he flew!

DAME TROT

Dame Trot and her
    cat
Sat down for to
    chat;
The Dame sat on
    this side,
And Puss sat on that.

" Puss," says the Dame,
" Can you catch a rat
Or a mouse in the dark?"
" Purr," says the cat.

IF

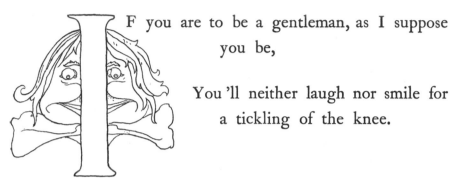

I F you are to be a gentleman, as I suppose
you be,

You'll neither laugh nor smile for
a tickling of the knee.

HOW DO YOU DO?

How do you do, neighbour?
Neighbour, how do you do?
Very well, I thank you.
How does Cousin Sue do?
She is very well,
And sends her love to you,
And so does Cousin Bell.
Ah! how, pray, does she
do?

THERE WAS A LITTLE BOY

There was a little boy and
    a little girl,
    Lived in an alley;
Says the little boy to the
    little girl,
    " Shall I, oh, shall I?"

Says the little girl to the
    little boy,
    " What shall we do?"

      Says the little boy to the little girl,
        " I will kiss you."

THE MAN IN THE WILDERNESS

The man in the wilderness
    asked me,

How many strawberries grew
    in the sea?

I answered him, as I thought
    good,

As many as red herrings
    grew in the wood.

THOMAS A' TATTAMUS

THOMAS A' TATTAMUS took
  two T's

To tie two tups to two tall
  trees,

To frighten the terrible Thomas
  A' Tattamus!

Tell me how many T's there
  are in all that.

LITTLE GIRL,
LITTLE GIRL

Little girl, little girl, where have you
  been?

Gathering roses to give to the Queen.

Little girl, little girl, what gave she
  you?

She gave me a diamond as big as
  my shoe.

LENGTHENING DAYS

As the days grow longer

The storms grow stronger

A MEDLEY

O N Christmas Eve I turned the
spit,
I burnt my fingers, I feel it
yet;
The cock sparrow flew over
the table,
The pot began to play with the ladle;
The ladle stood up like a naked man,
And vowed he'd fight the frying-pan;
The frying-pan behind the door
Said he never saw the like before;
And the kitchen clock I was going to wind
Said he never saw the like
behind.

THE WISE MEN OF GOTHAM

Three wise men of Gotham
They went to sea in a bowl;
And if the bowl had been
stronger,
My song had been longer.

WEE WILLIE WINKIE

WEE WILLIE WINKIE runs through the
town,

Up stairs and down stairs, in his night-
gown,

Rapping at the window, crying through
the lock:

"Are the children in their beds, for
it's past eight o'clock."

BAA, BAA, BLACK SHEEP

Baa, baa, black sheep, have you any wool?
Yes, marry, have I, three bags full:
One for my master, one for my dame,
But none for the little boy who cries in the lane.

EARLY RISING

E that would thrive,

Must rise at five;

He that hath thriven,

May lie till seven;

And he that by the plough
would thrive,

Himself must either hold or drive.

THE TAILORS AND THE SNAIL

Four and twenty tailors went to kill a snail,

The best man amongst them durst not touch her tail;

She put out her horns like a little Kyloe cow,

Run, tailors, run, or she'll kill you all e'en now.

OLD KING COLE

Old King Cole was a merry old soul,

And a merry old soul was he;

He called for his pipe,

And he called for his bowl,

And he called for his

fiddlers three.

Every fiddler, he had a fine fiddle,

And a very fine fiddle had he;

Twee tweedle dee, tweedle dee, went the fiddlers.

Old King Cole

Oh, there's none so rare,

As can compare

With King Cole

And his fiddlers three!

BUTTONS

BUTTONS, a farthing a pair,
    Come, who will buy them of me?
    They 're round and sound and pretty,
    And fit for the girls of the city.
    Come, who will buy them of me,
    Buttons, a farthing a pair?

SULKY SUE

Here 's Sulky Sue;
What shall we do?
Turn her face to the wall
Till she comes to.

HECTOR PROTECTOR

Hector Protector was dressed
    all in green;
Hector Protector was sent to
    the Queen.
The Queen did not like him,
No more did the King;
So Hector Protector was sent
    back again.

JERRY
AND JAMES AND
JOHN

HERE was an old woman had
    three sons,
Jerry and James and John;
Jerry was hung, James was
    drowned,
John was lost, and never was
    found;
And there was an end of her three sons,
Jerry and James and John!

The Old Woman
who lived in a Shoe

THE OLD WOMAN WHO LIVED IN A SHOE

THERE was an old woman who lived in a shoe,

She had so many children she didn't know what to do;

She gave them some broth without any bread,

Then whipped them all round, and sent them to bed.

NEEDLES AND PINS

Needles and pins, needles and pins,

When a man marries his trouble begins.

THE SONG OF MYSELF

As I walked by myself,
And talked to myself,
　　Myself said unto me:
Look to thyself,
Take care of thyself,
　　For nobody cares for thee.

I answered myself,
And said to myself,
　　In the self-same repartee:
Look to thyself,
Or not look to thyself,
　　The self-same thing will be.

TIT-TAT-TOE

IT-TAT-TOE,
My first go,
Three jolly butcher-boys
All of a row;
Stick one up,
Stick one down,
Stick one in the old man's crown.

TWINKLE, TWINKLE LITTLE STAR

TWINKLE, twinkle, little star,
How I wonder what you are!

128

Twinkle, twinkle, little Star

Up above the world so high,
Like a diamond in the sky.

When the blazing sun is gone,
When he nothing shines upon,
Then you show your little light,
Twinkle, twinkle, all the night.

Then the traveller in the dark
Thanks you for your tiny spark:
How could he see where to go,
If you did not twinkle so?

In the dark blue sky you keep,
Often through my curtains peep,
For you never shut your eye
Till the sun is in the sky.

How your bright and tiny spark
Lights the traveller in the dark!
Though I know not what you are,
Twinkle, twinkle, little star.

THE CODLIN WOMAN

There was a little woman, as I 've been told,
Who was not very young, nor yet very old,
Now this little woman her living got,
By selling codlins, hot, hot, hot!

OF PIGS

LONG-TAILED pig and a short-
    tailed pig,
  Or a pig without e'er a tail,
  A sow pig, or a boar pig,
  Or a pig with a curly tail.

130

GOOD KING ARTHUR

WHEN good King Arthur ruled this
land
He was a goodly king;
He stole three pecks of barley-meal
To make a bag-pudding.

Good King Arthur

A bag-pudding the
      king did make,
And stuff'd it well
      with plums;

Good King Arthur

And in it put great lumps of fat,
    As big as my two thumbs.

The king and queen did eat thereof,
    And noble men beside;
And what they could not eat that night,
    The queen next morning fried.

SOLOMON GRUNDY

OLOMON GRUNDY,
     Born on a Monday,
     Christened on Tuesday,
     Married on Wednesday,
     Took ill on Thursday,
     Worse on Friday,
     Died on Saturday,
     Buried on Sunday,
     This is the end
     Of Solomon Grundy.

THREE BLIND MICE

Three blind mice, three blind mice,
They all ran after the
     farmer's wife,
She cut off their tails with
     a carving knife;
Did you ever see such a
     thing in your life
As three blind mice?

CROSS-PATCH

CROSS-PATCH, draw the latch,
　　Sit by the fire and spin;
Take a cup, and drink it up,
　　Then call your neighbours in.

YANKEE DOODLE

Yankee Doodle came to town,
　　Mounted on a pony;
He stuck a feather in his cap
And called it Maccaroni.

Yankee Doodle came to town,
　　Yankee Doodle dandy,
He stuck a feather in his cap
And called it sugar-candy.

135

The WAY to LONDON TOWN.

EE-SAW, sacaradown,

Which is the way to London town?

One foot up, the other foot down,

That is the way to London town.

CÆSAR'S SONG

Bow, wow, wow, whose dog art thou?

Little Tom Tinker's dog,

Bow,

wow,

wow.

WASH ME AND COMB ME

Wash me and comb me,
And lay me down softly,
And lay me on a bank to
    dry,
That I may look pretty,
When somebody comes by.

TEN FINGERS

One, two, three, four, five,
Once I caught a fish alive,
Six, seven, eight, nine, ten,
But I let him go again.

Why did you let him go?
Because he bit my finger so.
Which finger did he bite?
The little one upon the right.

137

BOYS and GIRLS

Boys and girls come out to play,
The moon doth shine as bright as day;

Boys and Girls

Boys and Girls

Come with a whoop, and come with a call,
Come with a good will or come not at all.

Lose your supper and lose your sleep,
Come to your playfellows in the street.

Up the ladder and down the wall,
A halfpenny loaf will serve us all;

You find milk, and I'll find flour,
And we'll have a pudding in half an hour.

SING IVY

MY father he left me three acres of
    land,
    Sing ivy, sing ivy;
My father he left me three acres of land,
    Sing holly, go whistle, and ivy!

I ploughed it with a ram's horn,
    Sing ivy, sing ivy;
And sowed it all over with one pepper-
    corn,
    Sing holly, go whistle, and ivy!

I harrowed it with a bramble bush,
    Sing ivy, sing ivy;
And reaped it with my little pen-knife,
    Sing holly, go whistle, and ivy!

PUSSYCAT MEW

Pussycat Mew jumped over a coal,
And in her best petticoat burnt a
  great hole.

Poor Pussy 's weeping, she 'll have
  no more milk,
Until her best petticoat 's mended
  with silk!

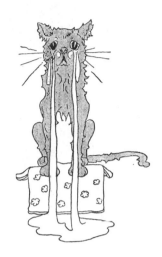

GOOSEY, GOOSEY, GANDER

OOSEY, goosey, gander,
  Whither dost thou wander?
  Up stairs and down stairs,
And in my lady's chamber.

There I met an old man
  That would not say his prayers;
I took him by the left leg,
  And threw him down stairs.

143

THE MAN AND HIS CALF

THERE was an old man,
And he had a calf,
And that's half;
He took him out of the stall,
And put him on the wall,
And that's all.

RIDE A COCK-HORSE

Ride a cock-horse
To Banbury Cross,
To see what Tommy can buy;
A penny white loaf,
A penny white cake,
And a twopenny
apple-pie.

SEEKING A WIFE

When I was a bachelor, I lived by myself,
And all the bread and cheese I got I put upon a shelf,
The rats and the mice did lead me such a life,
That I went up to London, to get myself a wife.

The streets were so broad, and the lanes were so narrow,
I could not get my wife home without a wheelbarrow,
The wheelbarrow broke, my wife got a fall,
Down tumbled wheelbarrow, little wife, and all.

DOCTOR FAUSTUS

DOCTOR FAUSTUS was a good
man,
He whipped his scholars now
and then;
When he whipped them he
made them dance
Out of Scotland into France,
Out of France into Spain,
And then he whipped them back again.

POLLY, PUT THE KETTLE ON

Polly, put the kettle on,
Polly, put the kettle on,
Polly, put the kettle on,
And we 'll have tea.
Sukey, take it off again,
Sukey, take it off again,
Sukey, take it off again,
They 're all gone away.

146

THE BLACKSMITH

ROBERT BARNES, fellow fine,
Can you shoe this horse of mine?"
"Yes, good sir, that I can,
As well as any other man;
Here's a nail, and there's a prod,
And now, good sir, your horse is shod."

THE FOUNT OF LEARNING

Here's A, B, and C, D, E, F, and G,
H, I, J, K, L, M, N, O, P, Q,
R, S, T, and U,
W, X, Y, and Z.
And here's the child's dad
Who is sagacious and discerning,
And knows this is the fount of all learning.

OF ARITHMETIC

MULTIPLICATION is vexation,
  Division is as bad;
The Rule of Three doth puzzle me,
  And Practice drives me mad.

OVER THE WATER
TO CHARLEY

Over the water, and over the lea,
And over the water to Charley.
Charley loves good ale and wine,
And Charley loves good brandy;
And Charley loves a pretty girl,
As sweet as sugar-candy.

Over the water, and over the sea,
And over the water to Charley,
I 'll have none of your nasty beef,
Nor I 'll have none of your barley;
But I 'll have some of your very best flour,
To make a white cake for my Charley.

148

Three Jolly Welshmen

Three Jolly Welshmen.

There were three jolly Welshmen,
As I have heard say,
And they went a-hunting
Upon St. David's day.

All the day they hunted,
And nothing could they find;

But a ship a-sailing,
  A-sailing with the wind.

One said it was a ship,
  The other he said "Nay";
The third he said it was a house,
  With the chimney blown away.

And all the night they hunted,
  And nothing could they find,
But the moon a-gliding,
  A-gliding with the wind.

One said it was the moon,
  The other he said "Nay";
The third he said it was a cheese,
  With half o' it cut away.

THE DAYS OF THE MONTH

THIRTY days hath September,
April, June, and November;
February has twenty-eight alone,
All the rest have thirty-one,
Except in leap-year, when's the time
That February has twenty-nine.

A VARIED SONG

I'll sing you a song,
The days are long,
The woodcock and the sparrow;
The little dog he has burned his tail,
And he must be hanged to-morrow.

152

A DILLER, A DOLLAR

A diller, a dollar,
A ten o'clock scholar;
What makes you come so soon?
You used to come at ten o'clock,
But now you come at noon.

A PIE SAT ON A PEAR-TREE

A PIE sat on a pear-tree,
 A pie sat on a pear-tree,
 A pie sat on a pear-tree,
 Heigh O, heigh O, heigh O!
Once so merrily hopped she,
 Twice so merrily hopped she,
 Thrice so merrily hopped she,
Heigh O, heigh O, heigh O!

THE GIRL IN THE LANE

The girl in the lane, that couldn't speak plain,

Cried gobble, gobble,
 gobble;

The man on the hill,
 that couldn't stand
 still,

Went hobble, hobble,
 hobble.

THREE MEN IN A TUB

Rub-a-dub-dub,

Three men in a tub;

And who do you think they be?

The butcher, the baker,

The candlestick-maker;

Turn 'em out, knaves all three!

155

LITTLE MISS MUFFET

ITTLE Miss Muffet,
> She sat on a tuffet,
> Eating of curds and whey;
> There came a big spider,
> And sat down beside her,
> And frightened Miss Muffet away.

THE BOY AND
THE OWL

There was a little boy
 went into a field,
 And lay down on
 some hay;

An owl came out and
 flew about,
 And the little boy ran
 away.

156

COCK ROBIN'S COURTING

Cock Robin got up early,
  At the break of day,
And went to Jenny's window
  To sing a roundelay.

He sang Cock Robin's love
  To the little Jenny Wren,
And when he got unto the end,
  Then he began again.

157

For EVERY EVIL

For every evil under the sun,
There is a remedy, or there is none.
If there be one, seek till you find it;
If there be none, never mind it.

WHEN I WAS A LITTLE BOY

When I was a little boy,
I washed my mammy's dishes,
I put my finger in
my eye,
And pulled out golden fishes.

ANDREW

A S I was going o'er Westminster Bridge,
 I met with a Westminster
  scholar;
He pulled off his cap, *an' drew*
 off his glove,
And wished me a very good
 morrow.
What is his name?

MARY'S CANARY

Mary had a pretty bird,
 Feathers bright and yellow;
Slender legs—upon my word,
 He was a pretty fellow.
The sweetest note he al-
 ways sung,
 Which much delighted
 Mary;
She often, where the cage
 was hung,
 Sat hearing her canary.

159

THE CUCKOO

In April,
Come he will.

In May,
He sings all day.

In June,
He changes his tune.

In July,
He prepares to fly.

In August,
Go he must.

A SWARM OF BEES

A swarm of bees in May
Is worth a load of hay;
A swarm of bees in June
Is worth a silver spoon;
A swarm of bees in July
Is not worth a fly.

ROBIN AND RICHARD

Robin and Richard were two little men,
They did not awake till the clock struck ten;

Then up starts Robin, and looks at the sky;
Oh! brother Richard, the sun's very high!

They both were ashamed, on such a fine day,
When they were wanted to make the new hay.

Do you go before, with bottle and bag,
I will come after on little Jack nag.

The Death and Burial of Cock Robin

The Death and Burial of Cock Robin

WHO killed Cock Robin?

"I" said the sparrow

"With my bow and arrow,
I killed Cock Robin."

WHO saw him die?

"I" said the fly

"With my little eye,
I saw him die."

HO caught his blood?

"With my little dish,
I caught his blood."

HO 'LL make his shroud?

"With my thread and needle,
I 'll make his shroud."

HO 'LL bear the torch?

"Will come in a minute,
I 'll bear the torch."

WHO 'LL be the clerk?

'I' said the lark

"I 'll say Amen in the dark;
I 'll be the clerk."

WHO 'LL dig his grave?

'I' said the owl

"With my spade and trowel,
I 'll dig his grave."

WHO 'LL be the parson?

'I' said the rook

"With my little book,
I 'll be the parson."

WHO 'LL be chief mourner?

'I'said the dove

"I mourn for my love;
I 'll be chief mourner."

WHO 'LL sing his dirge?

'I'said the thrush

"As I sing in a bush,
I 'll sing his dirge."

WHO 'LL carry his coffin?

'I' said the kite

"If it be in the night,
I 'll carry his coffin."

166

 HO 'LL toll the bell?

 " Because I can pull,
I 'll toll the bell."

The birds of the air

Fell sighing and
sobbing

When they heard the
bell toll

For poor Cock
Robin.

LADY-BIRD, LADY-BIRD

Lady-Bird, Lady-Bird, fly away home,

Your house is on fire, your children have gone,

All but one, that lies under a stone;

Fly thee home, Lady-Bird, ere it be gone.

THE LOVING BROTHERS

I love you well, my little brother,
    And you are fond of me;
Let us be kind to one another,
    As brothers ought to be.
You shall learn to play with me,
    And learn to use my toys;
And then I think that we shall be
    Two happy little boys.

168

NOTHING-AT-ALL

There was an old woman
called Nothing-at-all,

Who rejoiced in a dwelling
exceedingly small;

A man stretched his mouth
to its utmost extent,

And down at one gulp house and old woman went.

FORTUNE-TELLING BY CHERRY-STONES

One, I love; two, I love;
Three, I love, I say;
Four, I love with all
my heart;
Five, I cast away;
Six, he loves; seven,
she loves;
Eight, both love;
Nine, he comes; ten,
he tarries;
Eleven, he courts; and
twelve, he marries.

Little Bo peep

Little Bo-peep

Little Bo-Peep has lost her sheep,
  And can't tell where to find them;
Let them alone, and they'll come home,
  And bring their tails behind them.

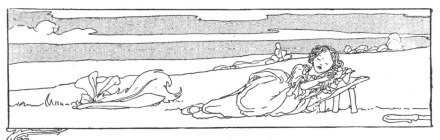

Little Bo-Peep fell fast asleep,
  And dreamt she heard them bleating;
And when she awoke, she found it a joke,
  For still they were all fleeting.

Then up she took her little
crook,

Determined for to find them;

Little Bo-Peep

She found them indeed, but it made her heart bleed,
    For they'd left all their tails behind them.

It happened one day as Bo-Peep did stray
    Into a meadow hard by,
There she espied their tails side by side,
    All hung on a tree to dry.

Little Bo-Peep

She heaved a sigh, and wiped her eye,
  And went over hill and dale, oh;
And tried what she could, as a shepherdess should,
  To tack to each sheep its tail, oh!

To Bed!

TO BED!

Come let's to bed,
  Says Sleepy-head;
Sit up a while, says Slow;
  Put on the pan,
  Says Greedy Nan,
Let's sup before
   we go.

OF GOING TO BED

Go to bed first,
   A golden purse;

Go to bed second,
A golden pheasant;

Go to bed third,
A golden bird.

THERE WAS A BUTCHER

There was a butcher cut his thumb,
When it did bleed, then blood did come.

There was a chandler making candle,
When he them stript, he did them handle.

There was a cobbler clouting shoon,
When they were mended, they were done.

There was a crow sat on a stone,
When he was gone, then there was none.

There was a horse going to the mill,
When he went on, he stood not still.

There was a lackey ran a race,
When he ran fast, he ran apace.

There was a monkey climbed a tree,
When he fell down, then down fell he.

There was a navy went into Spain,
When it return'd, it came again.

There was an old woman lived under a hill,
And if she's not gone, she lives there still.

WINTER·HAS·COME

Cold and raw
  the north
  wind doth blow,

  Bleak in a morning
    early;

All the hills are covered
    with snow,

  And winter 's now come
    fairly.

Monday's Child

M ONDAY'S child is fair of face,

Monday's Child

Tuesday's child is full

of grace,

Wednesday's child is full

of woe,

Thursday's child has far

to go,

Monday's Child

Friday's child is loving
and giving,

Saturday's child works hard
for its living,

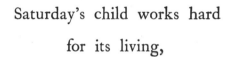

But the child that is born
on the Sabbath day

Is bonny, and blithe, and
good, and gay.

JACK
and
JILL

Jack and Jill
           went up the hill,
To fetch a
          pail of water.

Jack and Jill

Jack fell down, and
broke his crown,

And Jill
came tumbling
after.

Jack and Jill

Then up Jack got,
    and off did trot,
As fast as he
    could caper,

To old Dame Dob,
    who patched his nob,
With vinegar and
    brown paper.

185

CHARLEY
CHARLEY

C HARLEY, Charley, stole the barley

Out of the baker's shop,

The baker came out and gave him a
clout,

Which made poor Charley hop.

THE PIPER'S COW

There was a piper had a cow,
　　And he had nought to give her;
He pulled out his pipe, and played
　　　her a tune,
　　And bade the cow consider.

The cow considered very well,
　　And gave the piper a penny,
And bade him play the other tune—
　　"Corn rigs are bonny."

SHAVE A PIG

Barber, barber, shave a pig,

How many hairs will make a
　　wig?

"Four and twenty, that's
　　enough,"

Give the barber a pinch of
　　snuff.

187

TONGS

ONG legs, crooked thighs,

Little head, and no eyes.

GOING TO ST. IVES

As I was going to St. Ives
I met a man with seven wives;
Every wife had seven sacks,
Every sack had seven cats,
Every cat had seven kits.
Kits, cats, sacks, and wives,
How many were there going to St. Ives?

MERRY
are the BELLS

Merry are the bells, and merry would
    they ring;
Merry was myself, and merry could I
    sing;
With a merry ding-dong, happy, gay,
    and free,
And a merry sing-song, happy let us be!

Waddle goes your gait, and hollow are
    your hose;
Noddle goes your pate, and purple is
    your nose;
Merry is your sing-song, happy, gay,
    and free,
With a merry ding-dong, happy let us
    be!

Merry have we met, and merry have we
    been;
Merry let us part, and merry meet again;
With our merry sing-song, happy, gay,
    and free,
And a merry ding-dong, happy let us
    be!

MORE ABOUT
JACK JINGLE

NOW what do you think
Of little Jack Jingle?
Before he was married
He used to live single.

ROBIN, THE BOBBIN

Robin, the Bobbin, the bouncing Ben,

He ate more meat than four-score men;

He ate a cow, he ate a calf,

He ate a butcher and a half;

He ate a church, he ate a steeple,

He ate the priest, and all the people!

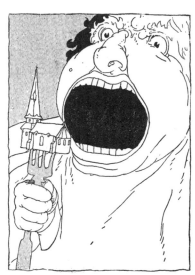

ALL FOR WANT OF A NAIL

For want of a nail, the shoe was lost,

For want of the shoe, the horse was lost,

For want of the horse, the rider was lost,

For want of the rider, the battle was lost,

For want of the battle, the kingdom was lost,

And all for the want of a horse-shoe nail!

CURLY LOCKS

Curly locks! curly locks!
    wilt thou be mine?
Thou shalt not wash dishes,
    nor yet feed the swine;
But sit on a cushion, and
    sew a fine seam,
And feed upon strawberries,
    sugar, and cream!

The King of France

THE King of France

Went up the hill,

W ITH twenty

thousand

men;

The King of France

came down

the hill,

And ne'er went up again.

THE LATEST NEWS

What
is
the
news
of
the
day,
Good
neighbour,
I
pray?

They
say
the
balloon
Is
gone
up
to
the
moon!

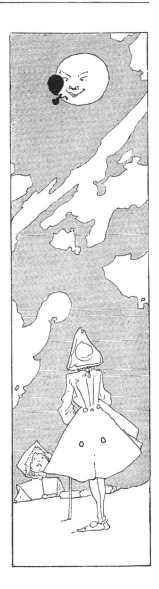

197

THE LIGHT-HEARTED FAIRY

Oh, who is so merry, so merry, heigh ho!
As the light-hearted fairy, heigh ho, heigh ho?
 He dances and sings
 To the sound of his wings,
With a hey, and a heigh, and a ho!

Oh, who is so merry, so merry, heigh ho!
As the light-hearted fairy, heigh ho, heigh ho?
 His nectar he sips
 From a primrose's lips,
With a hey, and a heigh, and a ho!

Oh, who is so merry, so merry, heigh ho!
As the light-footed fairy, heigh ho, heigh ho?
   His night is the noon,
   And his sun is the moon,
With a hey, and a heigh, and a ho!

I LIKE LITTLE PUSSY

I LIKE little Pussy, her coat is so
   warm,
   And if I don't hurt her she'll
     do me no harm;
   So I'll not pull her tail, nor drive
     her away,
   But Pussy and I very gently will
     play.

199

PUNCH AND JUDY

Punch and Judy
    Fought for a pie,
Punch gave Judy
    A knock in the eye.

Says Punch to Judy,
    " Will you have any more?"
Says Judy to Punch,
    " My eye is too sore."

The Obstinate Pig

The Obstinate Pig.

A N old woman was sweeping her house, and she found a little crooked sixpence.

"What," said she, " shall I do with this little sixpence? I will go to market, and buy a little pig."

As she was coming home she came to a stile; but Piggy would not go over the stile.

The Obstinate Pig

SHE went a little farther and she met a dog. So she said to the dog:

"Dog, dog, bite pig!
Piggy won't get over the
stile;
And I sha'n't get home
to-night."

But the dog would not.

SHE went a little farther and she met a stick. So she said:

"Stick, stick, beat dog!
Dog won't bite pig;
Pig won't get over the stile;
And I sha'n't get home to-night."

But the stick would not.

SHE went a little farther and she met a fire. So she said:

"Fire, fire, burn stick!
Stick won't beat dog;
Dog won't bite pig;
Pig won't get over the stile;
And I sha'n't get home to-
night."

But the fire would not.

The Obstinate Pig

HE went a little farther and she met some water. So she said:

"Water, water, quench fire!
Fire won't burn stick;
Stick won't beat dog;
Dog won't bite pig;
Pig won't get over the stile;
And I sha'n't get home to-night."

But the water would not.

HE went a little farther and she met an ox. So she said:

"Ox, ox, drink water!
Water won't quench fire;
Fire won't burn stick;
Stick won't beat dog;
Dog won't bite pig;
Pig won't get over the stile;
And I sha'n't get home to-night."

But the ox would not.

The Obstinate Pig

SHE went a little farther and she met a butcher. So she said:

"Butcher, butcher, kill ox!
Ox won't drink water;
Water won't quench fire;
Fire won't burn stick;
Stick won't beat dog;
Dog won't bite pig;
Pig won't get over the stile;
And I sha'n't get home to-night."

But the butcher would not.

SHE went a little farther and she met a rope. So she said:

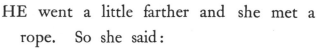

"Rope, rope, hang butcher!
Butcher won't kill ox;
Ox won't drink water;
Water won't quench fire;
Fire won't burn stick;
Stick won't beat dog;
Dog won't bite pig;

The Obstinate Pig

Pig won't get over the stile;
And I sha'n't get home to-night."

But the rope would not.

HE went a little farther and she met a rat. So
she said:

"Rat, rat, gnaw rope!
Rope won't hang
butcher;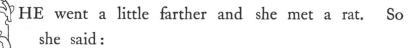
Butcher won't kill ox;
Ox won't drink water;
Water won't quench fire;
Fire won't burn stick;
Stick won't beat dog;
Dog won't bite pig;
Pig won't get over the stile;
And I sha'n't get home to-night."

But the rat would not.

The Obstinate Pig

SHE went a little farther and she met a cat. So she said:

"Cat, cat, kill rat!
Rat won't gnaw rope;
Rope won't hang butcher;
Butcher won't kill ox;
Ox won't drink water;
Water won't quench fire;
Fire won't burn stick;
Stick won't beat dog;
Dog won't bite pig;
Pig won't get over the stile;
And I sha'n't get home to-night."

The cat said: "If you will get me a saucer of milk from the cow in yonder field I will kill the rat."

So the old woman went to the cow and said: "Cow, cow, will you give me a saucer of milk?" And the cow said: "If you will get me a bucket full of water from yonder brook I will give you the milk." And the old woman took the bucket to the brook; but the water all rushed out through the holes in the bottom.

The Obstinate Pig

So she filled the holes up with stones, got the water, and took it to the cow, who at once gave her the saucer of milk. Then the old woman gave the cat the milk, and when she had lapped up the milk—

> The cat began to kill the rat;
> The rat began to gnaw the rope;
> The rope began to hang the butcher;
> The butcher began to kill the ox;
> The ox began to drink the water;
> The water began to quench the fire;
> The fire began to burn the stick;
> The stick began to beat the dog;
> The dog began to bite the pig;
> The pig jumped over the stile;
> And so the old woman got home that night.

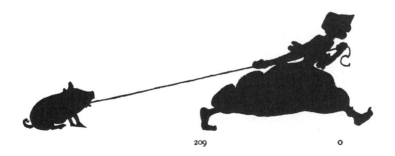

BOW-WOW, SAYS THE DOG

Bow-wow, says the dog;
　Mew-mew, says the cat;
Grunt, grunt, goes the hog;
　And squeak, goes the rat.

Chirp, chirp, says the sparrow;
　Caw, caw, says the crow;
Quack, quack, says the duck;
　And what cuckoos say, you
　　know.

So, with sparrows and cuckoos,
　With rats and with dogs,
With ducks and with crows,
　With cats and with hogs,

A fine song I have made,
　To please you, my dear;
And if it's well sung,
　'T will be charming to hear.

THE BURNY BEE

BLESS you, bless you, burny bee;

Say, when will your wedding
be?

If it be to-morrow day,

Take your wings and fly away.

DANTY BABY

Danty baby diddy,

What can mammy do wid 'e,

But sit in a lap,

And give 'un a pap?

Sing danty baby diddy.

THE DOVE AND THE WREN

THE Dove says, coo, coo, what shall I do?

I can scarce maintain two.

Pooh, pooh! says the wren, I have got ten,

And keep them all like gentlemen.

TOMMY'S CAKE

Pat-a-cake, pat-a-cake,
Baker's man!
That I will master,
As fast as I can.

Pat it, and prick it,
And mark it with T,
And there will be enough
For Jacky and me.

212

THE MAN OF THESSALY

There was a man of Thessaly,
    And he was wond'rous wise,
He jump'd into a quickset hedge,
    And scratched out both his eyes:

But when he saw his eyes were out,
    With all his might and main
He jump'd into another hedge,
    And scratch'd them back again.

CUSHY COW

Cushy cow, bonny, let down thy milk,
And I will give thee a gown of silk;
A gown of silk and a silver tee,
If thou wilt let down thy milk to me.

THERE WAS AN OLD WOMAN

THERE was an old woman, and
what do you think?
She lived upon nothing but
victuals and drink;
And tho' victuals and drink were
the chief of her diet,
This plaguy old woman could
never keep quiet.
She went to the baker to buy her
some bread,
And when she came home her
old husband was dead;
She went to the clerk to toll the bell,
And when she came back her old husband was well.

215

TELL-TALE-TIT

Tell-tale-tit,
Your tongue shall be slit,
And all the dogs in our town
Shall have a little bit.

ELIZABETH, ELSPETH, BETSY, AND BESS

Elizabeth, Elspeth, Betsy, and Bess,
They all went together to
seek a bird's nest.

They found a bird's
nest with five eggs
in,
They all took one
and left four in.

216

SING A SONG of SIXPENCE

ING a song of sixpence,
   Pockets full of rye;
Four and twenty black-
     birds
   Baked in a pie.

When the pie was opened
   The birds began to
     sing;
Was not that a dainty dish
   To set before the king?

Sing a Song of Sixpence

The king was in his counting-
house

Counting out his money;

The queen was in the parlour,

Eating bread and honey;

Sing a Song of Sixpence

The maid was in the garden
Hanging out the clothes,
Down came a blackbird,
And snapped off her nose.

THREE CHILDREN SLIDING

Three children sliding
   on the ice
  Upon a summer's day,
As it fell out, they all
   fell in,
    The rest
    they ran
    away.

O! had these children
  been at school,
  Or sliding on dry
   ground,
Ten thousand pounds to
  one penny
  They had not then
  been drown'd.

Three Children Sliding

Ye parents who have children dear,
   And eke ye that have none,
If you would have them safe abroad,
   Pray keep them safe at home.

RIDE AWAY, RIDE AWAY.

RIDE away, ride away,
Johnny shall ride,

And he shall have pussy-cat tied to one side;

And he shall have little dog tied to the other;

And Johnny shall ride to see his grandmother.

MOTHER GOOSE

LD Mother Goose, when
    She wanted to wander,
Would ride through the air
    On a very fine gander.

Mother Goose had a house,
    'T was built in a wood,
Where an owl at the door
    For sentinel stood.

She had a son Jack,
    A plain-looking lad,
He was not very good,
    Nor yet very bad.

224

She sent him to market,
  A live goose he bought;
" Here, Mother," says he,
  " It will not go for nought."

Jack's goose and her gander
  Grew very fond;
They 'd both eat together,
  Or swim in one pond.

Jack found one morning,
  As I have been told,
His goose had laid him
  An egg of pure gold.

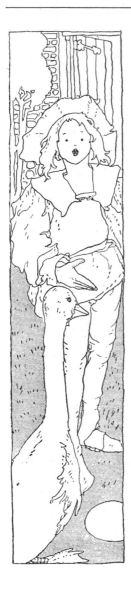

Jack ran to his mother,
   The news for to tell,
She called him a good boy,
   And said it was well.

Jack sold his gold egg
   To a rogue of a Jew,
Who cheated him out of
   The half of his due.

Then Jack went a-courting
   A lady so gay,
As fair as the lily,
   As sweet as the May.

The Jew and the Squire
Came behind his back,
And began to belabour
The sides of poor Jack.

Then old Mother Goose
That instant came in,
And turned her son Jack
Into famed Harlequin.

She then with her wand
Touched the lady so fine,
And turned her at once
Into sweet Columbine.

227

The gold egg into
  The sea was thrown then,—
When Jack jumped in,
  And got the egg back again.

The Jew got the goose,
  Which he vowed he would kill,
Resolving at once
  His pockets to fill.

Jack's mother came in,
  And caught the goose soon,
And mounting its back,
  Flew up to the moon.

DEAR, DEAR!

Dear, dear! what can the matter
    be?
Two old women got up in an
    apple-tree;

One came down,
And the other stayed till Satur-
    day.

THE LION AND THE UNICORN

The lion and the unicorn were fighting for the crown;
The lion beat the unicorn
    all round about the town.
Some gave them white bread,
    and some gave them brown;
Some gave them
    plum-cake,
    and sent them
    out of town.

THE LITTLE MOUSE

I HAVE seen you, little mouse,
  Running all about the house,
  Through the hole, your little eye
  In the wainscot peeping sly,
  Hoping soon some crumbs to steal,
To make quite a hearty meal.
Look before you venture out,
See if pussy is about,
If she 's gone, you 'll quickly run
To the larder for some fun,
Round about the dishes creep,
Taking into each a peep,
To choose the daintiest that 's there,
Spoiling things you do not care.

THE NUT-TREE

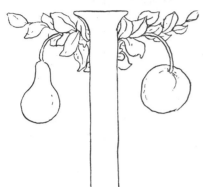

I HAD a little nut-tree, nothing would it bear

But a silver nutmeg and a golden pear;

The King of Spain's daughter came to see me,

And all was because of my little nut-tree.

I skipped over water, I danced over sea,

And all the birds in the air couldn't catch me.

POLLY FLINDERS

LITTLE Polly Flinders

Sat among the cinders,

Warming her ten little toes!

Her mother came and caught her,

And whipped her little daughter,

For spoiling her nice new clothes.

231

Brian O'Lin

BRIAN O'LIN

Brian O'Lin had no breeches to wear,
So he bought him a sheep-skin and made him a pair,
With the skinny side out, and the woolly side in,
"Ah, ha, that is warm!" said Brian O'Lin.

Brian O'Lin and his wife and wife's mother,
They all went over a bridge together;
The bridge was broken and they all fell in,
"Mischief take all!" quoth Brian O'Lin.

232

MARGERY DAW

SEE-SAW, MARGERY DAW,

Jacky shall have a new master.

He shall have but a penny a day,

Because he can't work any faster.

NONSENSE

We are all in the dumps,
For diamonds are trumps,
   The kittens are gone to St. Paul's,
The babies are bit,
The moon's in a fit,
   And the houses are built without walls.

ANOTHER FALLING OUT

MY little old man and I fell out;

I'll tell you what 't was all about:

I had money and he had none,

And that's the way the noise begun.

233

Little B°Y BLUE

LITTLE BOY BLUE, come, blow up your horn;
The sheep's in the meadow, the cow's in the corn.
Where's the little boy that looks after the sheep?
Under the haystack, fast asleep.

LITTLE TOM TUCKER

Little Tom Tucker sings for his supper.

What shall he eat? White bread and butter.

How will he cut it without e'er a knife?

How will he be married without e'er a wife?

OLD WOMAN, OLD WOMAN

"O LD woman, old woman, shall we go a-shearing?"

"Speak a little louder, sir, I'm very thick of hearing."

"Old woman, old woman, shall I kiss you dearly?"

"Thank you, kind sir, I hear you very clearly."

UP HILL AND
DOWN DALE

Up hill and down dale;
Butter is made in every vale;
And if that Nancy Cook
Is a good girl,
She shall have a spouse,
And make butter anon,
Before her old grandmother
Grows a young man.

236

LUCY LOCKET

Lucy Locket
Lost her pocket,
Kitty Fisher
Found it;
Nothing in it,
Nothing in it,
But the binding
Round it.

FORTUNE-TELLING BY DAISY PETALS

He loves me, he don't!
He 'll have me, he won't!

He would if he could,
But he can't, so he don't!

237

BABY BUNTING

BABY, baby bunting,
  Father 's gone a-hunting,

  Mother 's gone a-milking,
  Sister 's gone a-silking,

Brother 's gone to buy a skin
To wrap the baby bunting in.

THE MOUSE RAN up the CLOCK

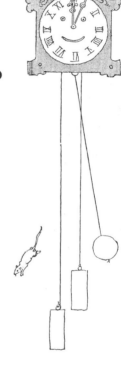

Dickory,
    Dickory,
        Dock!
The mouse ran up
    the clock,
The clock struck
    one,
The mouse ran
    down,
Dickory,
    Dickory,
        Dock!

ONE MISTY MOISTY MORNING.

One misty, moisty morning, when cloudy was the weather,

There I met an old man clothed all in leather;

He began to compliment and I began to grin,

How do you do? how do you do? how do you do again?

THE LITTLE HUSBAND

I HAD a little husband,
  No bigger than my thumb;
I put him in a pint pot,
  And then I bade him drum.

I bought a little horse,
  That galloped up and down;
I bridled him, and saddled him,
  And sent him out of town.

I gave him a pair of garters
  To tie up his little hose,
And a little silk handkerchief
  To wipe his little nose.

TO THE HAYFIELD

Willy boy, Willy boy, where
  are you going?
I will go with you, if that
  I may.
I'm going to the meadow
  to see them a-mowing,
I'm going to help them
  make the hay.

THE MONTHS OF THE YEAR

JANUARY brings the snow,
  Makes our feet and fingers
    glow.

February brings the rain,
Thaws the frozen lake again.

March brings breezes, loud
    and shrill,
  To stir the dancing daffodil.

April brings the primrose
    sweet,
Scatters daisies at our feet.

242

Months of the Year

May brings flocks of pretty
    lambs,

Skipping by their fleecy dams.

June brings tulips, lilies, roses,

Fills the children's hands
    with posies.

Hot July brings cooling
    showers,

Apricots, and gillyflowers.

August brings the sheaves of
    corn,

Then the harvest home is
    borne.

Months of the Year

Warm September brings the fruit;

Sportsmen then begin to shoot.

Fresh October brings the pheasant;

Then to gather nuts is pleasant.

Dull November brings the blast;

Then the leaves are whirling fast.

Chill December brings the sleet,

Blazing fire, and Christmas treat.

THE LITTLE MOPPET

HAD a little moppet,

    I put it in my pocket,

And fed it with corn and hay,

    There came a proud beggar

    And swore he would have her,

And stole my little moppet away.

SIMON BRODIE'S COW

IMON BRODIE had a cow;

    He lost his cow and could not find her;

    When he had done what man could do,

The cow came home and her tail behind her.

A
CARRION
CROW

A carrion crow sat on an oak,

    Fol de riddle, lol de riddle, hi ding do,

Watching a tailor shape his cloak;

Sing heigh ho, the carrion crow,
Fol de riddle, lol de riddle, hi ding do.

A Carrion Crow

Wife, bring me my old
bent bow,

Fol de riddle, lol de
riddle, hi ding do,

That I may shoot yon car-
rion crow;

Sing heigh ho, the
carrion crow,

Fol de riddle, lol de
riddle, hi ding do.

The tailor he shot and
missed his mark,

Fol de riddle, lol de riddle, hi ding do,

A Carrion Crow

And shot his own sow quite through the heart;
    Sing heigh ho, the carrion crow,
    Fol de riddle, lol de riddle, hi ding do.

Wife, bring brandy in a spoon,
    Fol de riddle, lol de riddle, hi ding do,
For our old sow is in a swoon,
    Sing heigh ho, the carrion crow,
    Fol de riddle, lol de riddle, hi ding do.

NANNY ETTICOAT

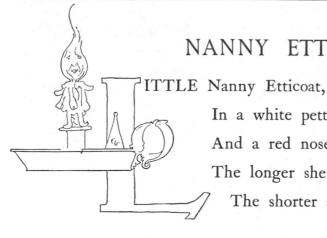

LITTLE Nanny Etticoat,
    In a white petticoat
    And a red nose;
    The longer she stands
       The shorter she grows.

GOOD-FRIDAY SONG

Hot-cross Buns!
Hot-cross Buns!
One a penny, two a penny,
    Hot-cross Buns!

Hot-cross Buns!
Hot-cross Buns!
If ye have no daughters,
    Give them to your
    sons.

250

I·SAW·A·SHIP·A·SAILING·

I SAW a ship a-sailing,
    A-sailing on the sea;
And it was full of pretty things
    For baby and for me.

There were sweetmeats in the cabin,
    And apples in the hold;
The sails were made of silk,
    And the masts were made of gold.

The four-and-twenty sailors
    That stood between the decks,
Were four-and-twenty white mice,
    With chains about their necks.

252

I saw a Ship a-sailing

The captain was a duck,

    With a packet on his back;

And when the ship began to move,

    The captain cried, " Quack, quack!"

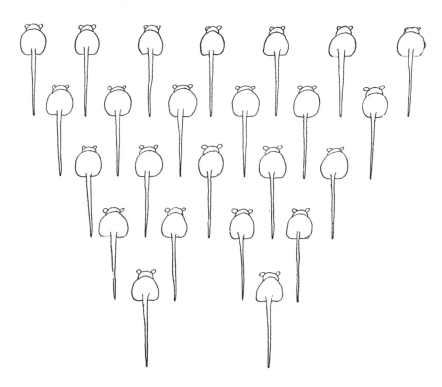

LITTLE ROBIN REDBREAST

Little Robin Redbreast sat upon
    a tree;

Up went Pussy cat and down
    went he.

Down came Pussy cat, and away
    Robin ran;

Says little Robin Redbreast: "Catch
    me if you can."

DIDDLE DIDDLE DUMPLING

DIDDLE diddle dumpling, my son John,

Went to bed with his breeches on,

One stocking off, and one stocking
    on;

Diddle diddle dumpling, my son
    John.

JACK JINGLE

ACK JINGLE went 'prentice
    To make a horse-shoe,
He wasted the iron
    Till it would not do.
His master came in,
    And began for to rail;
Says Jack, " the shoe 's spoiled,
    But 't will still make a nail."

He tried at the nail,
    But, chancing to miss,
Says, " If it won't make
      a nail,
    It shall yet make a
      hiss."
Then into the water
    Threw the hot iron,
      smack!
" Hiss!" quoth the iron;
    " I thought. so," says
      Jack.

ONE, TWO,

One, two,
Buckle my shoe;

Three, four,
Knock at the door;

Five, six,
Pick up sticks;

Seven, eight,
Lay them straight;

Nine, ten,
A good fat hen;

Eleven, twelve,
Who will delve;

Thirteen, fourteen,
Maids a-courting;

256

15.16.
17.18.
19.20.

Fifteen, sixteen,
Maids in the kitchen;

Seventeen, eighteen,
Maids a-waiting;

Nineteen, twenty,
My plate 's empty.

BETTY WINKLE'S PIG

Little Betty Winkle she had a little pig.
It was a little pig, not very big;
When he was alive he lived in Clover,
But now he 's dead, and that 's all over.
  Johnny Winkle he
   Sat down and cried;
  Betty Winkle she
   Lay down and died;
So there was an end of one, two, and three,
  Johnny Winkle he,
  Betty Winkle she,
  And Piggy Wiggie!

Three Brethren out of Spain

THREE BRETHREN OUT OF SPAIN

" We are three brethren out of Spain,
Come to court your daughter Jane."
" My daughter Jane she is too young;
She has no skill in a flattering tongue."

" Be she young, or be she old,
It 's for her gold she must be sold;
So fare you well, my lady gay,
We 'll call again another day."

" Turn back, turn back, thou scornful knight,
And rub thy spurs till they be bright."
" Of my spurs take you no thought,
For in this land they were not bought.
So fare you well, my lady gay,
We 'll call again another day."

" Turn back, turn back, thou scornful knight,
And take the fairest in your sight."
" The fairest maid that I can see
Is pretty Nancy; come to me."

WHAT CARE I?

What care I how black I be?
Twenty pounds shall marry
me.
If twenty won't, forty shall,
For I 'm my mother's bouncing
girl.

The THREE KITTENS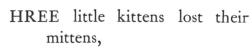

 HREE little kittens lost their
mittens,

And they began to cry,

" Oh, Mother dear,

We very much fear

That we have lost our mittens!"

" Lost your mittens!

You naughty kittens!

Then you shall have no pie.

Mee-ow, mee-ow, mee-ow!

No, you shall have no pie.

Mee-ow, mee-ow, mee-ow!"

The Three Kittens

The three little kittens found their mittens,
And they began to cry,
" Oh, Mother dear,
See here, see here,
See, we have found our mittens!"

" Put on your mittens,
You silly kittens,
And you shall have some pie.
Purr-r, purr-r, purr-r!"
" Oh, let us have the pie!
Purr-r, purr-r, purr-r!"

The Three Kittens

The three little kittens put on
    their mittens,
And soon ate up the pie;
    "Oh, Mother dear,
    We greatly fear
That we have soiled our mittens!"

"Soiled your mittens!
You naughty kittens!"
Then they began to sigh,
    Mi-ow, mi-ow, mi-ow!
Then they began to sigh,
    Mi-ow, mi-ow, mi-ow!

The Three Kittens

The three little kittens washed
    their mittens,
And hung them up to dry;
    " Oh, Mother dear,
    Do you not hear
That we have washed our mittens!"

    " Washed your mittens!
    Oh, you 're good kittens!
But I smell a rat close by.
    Hush! hush! mee-ow, mee-ow."
" We smell a rat close by,
    Mee-ow, mcc-ow, mcc-ow!"

THE LADY AND THE SWINE

There was a lady loved a swine,
    Honey, quoth she,
Pig-hog, wilt thou be mine?
    " Hoogh," quoth he.

I 'll build thee a silver stye,
    Honey, quoth she;
And in it thou shalt lie;
    " Hoogh!" quoth he.

Pinned with a silver pin,
    Honey, quoth she,
That thou mayst go out and in;
    " Hoogh!" quoth he.

Wilt thou now have me,
    Honey? quoth she;
" Hoogh, hoogh, hoogh!" quoth he,
    And went his way.

THE JOLLY MILLER

THERE was a jolly miller once
    Lived on the River Dee.
He worked and sang from morn till
    night,
    No lark so blithe as he;
And this the burden of his song
    For ever used to be:
"I care for nobody! no, not I!
And nobody cares for me!"

FEETIKINS

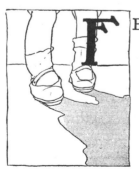

FEETIKIN, feetikin,
    When will ye gang?"
"When the nichts turn short,
    And the days turn lang,
I'll toddle and gang,
    Toddle and gang!"

TOM THE PIPER'S SON

Tom, Tom, the piper's son,
He learned to play when he was young,
But all the tune that he could play
Was "Over the hills and far away".
Over the hills, and a great way off,
And the wind will blow my top-knot off.

Now Tom with his pipe made such a noise
That he pleased both the girls and boys,
And they stopped to hear him play
"Over the hills and far away".

Tom with his pipe did play with such skill
That those who heard him could never stand still;
Whenever they heard they began for to dance,
Even pigs on their hind-legs would after him prance.

Tom the Piper's Son

As Dolly was milking the cow one day,
Tom took out his pipe and began for to play;
So Doll and the cow danced "the Cheshire round",
Till the pail was broke, and the milk ran on the ground.

He met old Dame Trot with a basket of eggs,
He used his pipe, and she used her legs;
She danced about till the eggs were all broke,
She began for to fret, but he laughed at the joke.

He saw a cross fellow was beating an ass,
Heavy laden with pots, pans, dishes, and glass;
He took out his pipe and played them a tune,
And the jack-ass's load was lightened full soon.

DOCTOR FELL

I do not like thee, Doctor
Fell;
The reason why I cannot
tell.
But this I know, and know
full well,
I do not like thee, Doctor
Fell.

THE FIFTH OF
NOVEMBER

PLEASE to remember
The fifth of November,
Gunpowder treason and plot.
I see no reason
Why gunpowder treason
Should ever be forgot.
Guy, Guy, Guy,
Stick him up on high,
Put him on the bonfire,
And there let him die.

271

BILLY, BILLY

BILLY, Billy, come and play,
  While the sun shines bright as day."

"Yes, my Polly, so I will,
  For I love to please you still."

"Billy, Billy, have you seen
  Sam and Betsy on the green?"

"Yes, my Poll, I saw them pass,
  Skipping o'er the new-mown grass."

"Billy, Billy, come along,
  And I will sing a pretty song."

"O then, Polly, I'll make haste,
  Not one moment
    will I waste,
But will come
  and hear you
    sing,
And my fiddle
  I will bring."

JOHNNY

Johnny shall have a new bonnet,
And Johnny shall go to the fair,
And Johnny shall have a blue ribbon
To tie up his bonny brown hair.

And why may not I love Johnny?
And why may not Johnny love me?
And why may not I love Johnny
As well as another body?

And here's a leg for a stocking,
And here's a foot for a shoe,
And he has a kiss for his daddy,
And two for his mammy, I trow.

And why may not I love Johnny?
And why may not Johnny love
me?
And why may not I love Johnny
As well as another body?

SING,
SING,

Sing, sing! what shall I sing?

The cat's run away with the pudding-bag string.

Do, do, what shall I do?

The cat has bit it quite in two.

PETER PIPER

PETER PIPER picked a peck of pickled pepper,
A peck of pickled pepper Peter Piper picked;
If Peter Piper picked a peck of pickled pepper,
Where 's the peck of pickled pepper Peter Piper picked?

NANCY DAWSON

Nancy Dawson was so fine
She wouldn't get up to serve the swine,
She lies in bed till eight or nine,
So its oh! poor Nancy Dawson.

And do you ken Nancy Dawson, honey?
The wife who sells the barley, honey?
She won't get up to feed her swine,
And do you ken Nancy Dawson, honey?

275

THE FARMER AND HIS DAUGHTER

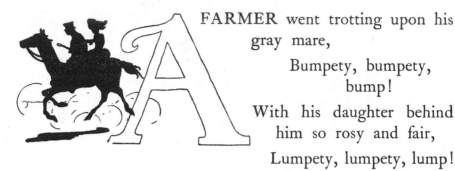

A FARMER went trotting upon his gray mare,
    Bumpety, bumpety, bump!
With his daughter behind him so rosy and fair,
    Lumpety, lumpety, lump!

A raven cried " croak " and they all tumbled down,
    Bumpety, bumpety, bump!
The mare broke her knees, and the farmer his crown,
    Lumpety, lumpety, lump!

The mischievous raven flew laughing away,
    Bumpety, bumpety, bump!
And vowed he would serve them the same the next day,
    Lumpety, lumpety, lump!

276

A STRANGE SIGHT.

UPON St. Paul's steeple stands a tree,
As full of apples as may be;
The little boys of London Town,
They run with hooks and pull them
    down;
And then they run from hedge to hedge,
Until they come to London Bridge.

I'LL TRY

Two Robin Redbreasts built their nest
   Within a hollow tree;
The hen sat quietly at home,
   The cock sang merrily;
And all the little ones said:
   "Wee, wee, wee, wee, wee, wee."

One day the sun was warm and bright,
   And shining in the sky,
Cock Robin said: "My little dears,
   'T is time you learned to fly;"
And all the little young ones said:
   "I'll try, I'll try, I'll try."

I know a child, and who she is
   I'll tell you by and by,
When Mamma says "Do this," or "that,"
   She says "What for?" and "Why?"
She'd be a better child by far
   If she would say "I'll try."

MASTER
I HAVE

Master I have, and I am his man,
    Gallop a dreary dun;
Master I have, and I am his man,
And I'll get a wife as fast as I can;
With a heighty gaily gamberally,
    Higgledy, piggledy, niggledy, niggledy,
      Gallop a dreary dun.

ROCK-A-BY, BABY

ROCK-A-BY, baby, thy cradle is green;
    Father's a nobleman, mother's a
      queen;
    And Betty's a lady, and wears a
      gold ring;
    And Johnny's a drummer, and
      drums for the king.

London Bridge

London Bridge

London Bridge is broken down,
  Dance o'er my Lady Lee;
London Bridge is broken down,
  With a gay lady.

How shall we build it up again?
  Dance o'er my Lady Lee;
How shall we build it up again?
  With a gay lady.

Silver and gold will be stole away,
  Dance o'er my Lady Lee;
Silver and gold will be stole away,
  With a gay lady.

London Bridge

Build it up again with iron and steel,
    Dance o'er my Lady Lee;
Build it up with iron and steel,
    With a gay lady.

Iron and steel will bend and bow,
    Dance o'er my Lady Lee;
Iron and steel will bend and bow,
    With a gay lady.

Build it up with wood and clay,
    Dance o'er my Lady Lee;
Build it up with wood and clay,
    With a gay lady.

Wood and clay will wash away,
    Dance o'er my Lady Lee;
Wood and clay will wash away,
    With a gay lady.

Build it up with stone so strong,
    Dance o'er my Lady Lee;
Huzza! 't will last for ages long,
    With a gay lady.

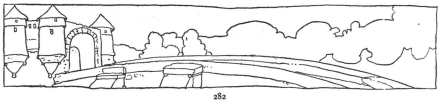

The FOX and the GOOSE

THE fox and his wife they had a great strife,

They never ate mustard in all their whole life;

They ate their meat without fork or knife,

    And loved to be picking a bone, e-ho!

The Fox and the Goose

The fox jumped up on a moonlight night;
The stars they were shining, and all things bright;
"Oh, ho!" said the fox, "it's a very fine night
    For me to go through the town, e-ho!"

The fox when he came to yonder stile,
He lifted his lugs and he listened a while;
"Oh, ho!" said the fox, "it's but a short mile
    From this into yonder wee town, e-ho!"

The Fox and the Goose

The fox when he came to the farmer's gate,
Whom should he see but the farmer's drake;
" I love you well for your master's sake,
    And long to be picking your bones, e-ho!"

The gray goose she ran round the hay-stack;
" Oh, ho!" said the fox, " you are very fat,
You 'll grease my beard and ride on my back
    From this into yonder wee town, e-ho!"

The farmer's wife she jumped out of bed,
And out of the window she popped her head;
" Oh, husband! oh, husband! the geese are all dead,
    For the fox has been through the town, e-ho!"

Then the old man got up in his red cap,
And swore he would catch the fox in a trap;
But the fox was too cunning, and gave him the slip,
    And ran through the town, the town, e-ho!

The Fox and the Goose

When he got to the top of the hill,
He blew his trumpet both loud and shrill,
For joy that he was in safety still,
    And had got away through the town, e-ho!

When the fox came back to his den,
He had young ones both nine and ten;
" You 're welcome home, daddy; you may go again,
    If you bring us such fine meat from the town,
        e-ho!"

WHERE ARE YOU GOING?

WHERE are you going to, my pretty
maid?"

"I'm going a-milking, sir,"
she said.

Where are you going?

"May I go with you, my pretty maid?"
"You 're kindly welcome, sir," she said.

"What is your father, my pretty maid?"
"My father 's a farmer, sir," she said.

"What is your fortune, my pretty maid?"
"My face is my fortune, sir," she said.

"Then I can't marry you, my pretty maid!"
"Nobody asked you, sir," she said.

KING PIPPIN'S HALL

KING PIPPIN built a fine new hall,
Pastry and pie-crust were the wall;
Windows made of black pudding
and white,
Slates were pancakes, you ne'er
saw the like.

IF

If all the world were apple-
pie,
And all the water ink,
What should we do for bread
and cheese?
What should we do for
drink?

COFFEE AND TEA

MOLLY, my sister, and I
fell out,
And what do you think
it was about?
She loved coffee and I
loved tea,
And that was the reason we couldn't agree.

THE CROOKED SONG

THERE was a crooked man, and he
went a crooked mile,

He found a crooked sixpence beside
a crooked stile;

He bought a crooked cat, which
caught a crooked mouse,

And they all lived together in a
little crooked house.

A, B, C

A, B, C, tumble down D,

The cat 's in the cupboard

And can't see me.

· COMICAL · FOLK

IN a cottage in Fife
Lived a man and his
  wife,
Who, believe me, were
  comical folk;
For, to people's surprise,
They both saw with their
  eyes,
And their tongues moved whenever they spoke.

When they were asleep,
I'm told—that to keep
Their eyes open they could not contrive;
They both walked on their feet,
And 't was thought what they eat
Helped, with drinking, to keep them alive.

A WONDERFUL THING

As I went to Bonner,

I met a pig

Without a wig,

Upon my word and

honour.

MY BOY TAMMIE

"WHERE have you been
all day,
My boy Tammie?"
"I've been all the day
Courting of a lady gay;
But oh, she's too young
To be taken from her mammy!"

"What work can she do,
  My boy Tammie?
Can she bake and can she brew,
  My boy Tammie?"

"She can brew and she can bake,
And she can make our wedding cake;
But oh, she's too young
To be taken from her mammy!"

"What age may she be?
What age may she be,
  My boy Tammie?"

"Twice two, twice seven,
Twice ten, twice eleven;
But oh, she's too young
To be taken from her mammy!"

THE LITTLE MAN WITH A GUN

There was a little man, and he had a little gun,
　And his bullets were made of lead, lead, lead;
He went to the brook, and saw a little duck,
　And shot it right through the head, head, head.

He carried it home to his old wife Joan,
　And bade her a fire to make, make, make,
To roast the little duck he had shot in the brook,
　And he 'd go and fetch the drake, drake, drake.

The drake was a-swimming, with his curly tail;
　The little man made it his mark, mark, mark.
He let off his gun, but he fired too soon,
　And the drake flew away with a quack, quack, quack.

IF WISHES

WERE HORSES

wishes were horses, beggars would ride;

If turnips were watches, I would wear
one by my side.

CLAP HANDIES

Clap, clap handies,
Mammie's wee, wee ain;
Clap, clap handies,
Daddie's comin' hame;
Hame till his bonny
wee bit laddie;
Clap, clap handies,
My wee, wee ain.

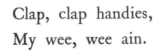

Taffy was a Welshman

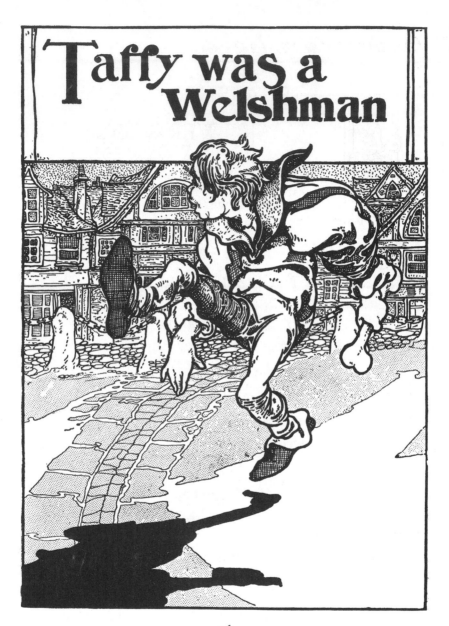

Taffy the Welshman

Taffy was a Welshman, Taffy was a thief;
Taffy came to my house and stole a piece of beef;
I went to Taffy's house, Taff was not at home;
Taffy came to my house and stole a marrow bone.

I went to Taffy's house, Taffy was not in;
Taffy came to my house and stole a silver pin;
I went to Taffy's house, Taffy was in bed,
I took up the beef bone and flung it at his head.

THERE WAS A MAN

THERE was a man, and he had naught,
  And robbers came to rob him;
He crept up to the chimney pot,
  And then they thought they had
    him.

But he got down on t' other side,
  And then they could not find him;
He ran fourteen miles in fifteen days,
  And never looked behind him.

JACK'S FIDDLE

Jacky, come give me thy fiddle,
  If ever thou mean to thrive.
Nay, I 'll not give my fiddle
  To any man alive.

If I should give my fiddle
  They 'll think that I 'm gone mad;
For many a joyful day
  My fiddle and I have had.

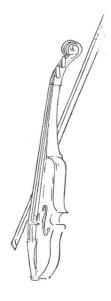

A was an archer

was an Archer, and shot at a Frog

was a Butcher, and kept a Bull-dog

was a Captain, all covered with Lace

was a Drunkard, and had a Red Face

was an Esquire, with insolent Brow

was a Farmer, and followed the Plough

was a Gamester, who had but Ill Luck

was a Hunter, and hunted a Buck

was an Innkeeper, who loved to Bouse

was a Joiner, and built up a House

was King William, once governed this Land

was a Lady, who had a White Hand

was a Miser, and hoarded up Gold

 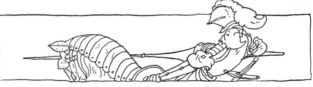

was a Nobleman, Gallant and Bold

302

was an Oyster Wench, and went about Town

was a Parson, and wore a Black Gown

was a Queen, who was fond of good Flip

was a Robber, and wanted a Whip

was a Sailor, and spent all he got

was a Tinker, and mended a Pot

was a Usurer, a miserable Elf

was a Vintner, who drank all Himself

was a Watchman, and guarded the Door

was Expensive, and so became Poor

was a Youth, that did not love School

was a Zany, a silly old Fool

THREE SHIPS

I SAW three ships come sailing by,
    Sailing by, sailing by,
I saw three ships come sailing by,
    On New-Year's day in the morning?

And what do you think was in them then,
    In them then, in them then?
And what do you think was in them then,
    On New-Year's day in the morning?

Three pretty girls were in them then,
    In them then, in them then,
Three pretty girls were in them then,
    On New-Year's day in the morning.

And one could whistle, and one could sing,
    And one could play on the violin,
Such joy there was at my wedding,
    On New-Year's day in the morning.

DING, DONG, BELL.

Ding, dong, bell, the cat is in the well!
Who put her in? Little Johnny Green.

Who pulled her out?

Little Tommy Stout.

What a naughty boy was that,

To try to drown poor pussy cat,

Who never did him any harm,

But killed the mice in his father's barn!

BOBBY SNOOKS

LITTLE BOBBY SNOOKS was fond of his books,

And loved by his usher and master;

But naughty Jack Spry, he got a black eye,

And carries his nose in a plaster.

308

SIX LITTLE MICE

Six little mice sat down to spin,
Pussy passed by, and she peeped in.
" What are you at, my little men?"
" Making coats for gentlemen."
" Shall I come in and bite off your threads?"
" No, no, Miss Pussy, you 'll bite off our heads."
" Oh, no, I 'll not, I 'll help you spin."
" That may be so, but you don't come in."

WING, WANG, WADDLE, OH

MY father he died, but I can't tell you how,
He left me six horses to drive in my plough;
    With my wing, wang, waddle, oh,
    Jack sing saddle, oh,
    Blowsey boys buble, oh,
    Under the broom.

I sold my six horses and I bought me a cow,
I'd fain have made a fortune but did not know how:
    With my wing, wang, waddle, oh,
    Jack sing saddle, oh,
    Blowsey boys buble, oh,
    Under the broom.

I sold my cow, and I bought me a calf;
I'd fain have made a fortune but lost the best half;

With my wing, wang, waddle, oh,
Jack sing saddle, oh,
Blowsey boys buble, oh,
Under the broom.

I sold my calf, and I bought me a cat;
A pretty thing she was, in my chimney corner sat;
With my wing, wang, waddle, oh,
Jack sing saddle oh,
Blowsey boys buble, oh,
Under the broom.

I sold my cat and bought me a mouse;
He carried fire in his tail, and burnt down my house;
With my wing, wang, waddle, oh,
Jack sing saddle, oh,
Blowscy boys buble, oh,
Under the broom.

THE HART

 THE hart he loves the high wood,

The hare she loves the hill;

The Knight he loves his bright
sword,

The Lady—loves her will.

OLD CHAIRS TO MEND

IF I'd as much money as I could
spend,
I never would cry old chairs to
mend;
Old chairs to mend, old chairs
to mend;
I never would cry old chairs to
mend.

If I'd as much money as I could
tell,
I never would cry old clothes to
sell;
Old clothes to sell, old clothes to sell;
I never would cry old clothes to sell.

SEE, SEE!

See, see! what shall I see?
A horse's head where his tail
should be!

Old Mother Hubbard

Mother Hubbard's old dog Tray,

If this account be true, Had not an equal, I dare say,

Come tell me, what think you?

Old Mother Hubbard

O LD Mother Hubbard
Went to her cupboard,
    To give her poor dog a bone;

When she came there
The cupboard was bare,
    And so the poor dog had none.

She went to the baker's
    To buy him some bread,
When she came back
    The dog was dead!

She went to the undertaker's
    To buy him a coffin;
When she came back
    The dog was laughing.

She took a clean dish
    To get him some tripe;
When she came back
    He was smoking his pipe.

Old Mother Hubbard

She went to the ale-house
    To get him some beer;
When she came back
    The dog sat in a chair.

She went to the tavern
    For white wine and red;
When she came back
    The dog stood on his head.

She went to the hatter's
    To buy him a hat;
When she came back
    He was feeding the cat.

She went to the barber's
　　To buy him a wig;
When she came back
　　He was dancing a jig.

She went to the fruiterer's
　　To buy him some fruit;
When she came back
　　He was playing the flute.

She went to the tailor's
　　To buy him a coat;
When she came back
　　He was riding a goat.

317

Old Mother Hubbard

She went to the cobbler's
    To buy him some shoes;
When she came back
    He was reading the news.

She went to the sempster's
    To buy him some linen;
When she came back
    The dog was spinning.

She went to the hosier's
    To buy him some hose;
When she came back
    He was dressed in his clothes.

The dame made a curtsy,
    The dog made a bow;
The dame said, "Your servant,"
    The dog said, "Bow-wow!"

TO BABYLON

HOW many miles is it to Babylon?

 Threescore miles and ten.

Can I get there by candle-light?

 Yes, and back again!

If your heels are nimble and light,

 You may get there by candle-light.

MY BLACK HEN

Hickety, pickety, my black
 hen,

She lays eggs for gentlemen;

Gentlemen come every day

To see what my black hen
 doth lay.

319

I'LL TELL YOU A STORY

I'll tell you a story
About Jack a Nory—
And now my story's begun:

I'll tell you another,
About Jack his brother—
And now my story's done.

WALTER JERROLD (1865–1929) was born in Liverpool but spent most of his life in London, where he followed a literary career. Starting work as a clerk in a newspaper counting-house, he went on to become deputy editor of *The Observer*. He edited many classic texts for the newly founded Everyman's Library, he wrote biographies, he produced stories for children under the name of Walter Copeland. In 1895 he married Clara Armstrong and his five daughters were obviously a ready audience and true inspiration for his bumper collection of nursery rhymes. While explaining that this was based on earlier collections made by John Newbery, Joseph Ritson and James Orchard Halliwell, he admitted that 'Tradition in the nursery has acted as a severe editor . . .'

CHARLES ROBINSON (1870–1937) was the second of the three artist sons of a wood engraver. Born in Camden Town, north London, he was apprenticed to the lithographers, Waterlow & Son, while an evening student at Heatherley's School of Art. In 1892 he began freelancing from his father's studio in the Strand and came to the notice of the publisher John Lane, who commissioned him to illustrate R.L. Stevenson's *A Child's Garden of Verses* for The Bodley Head. The book's success established him as an artist with an instinctive feeling for book design and thereafter he never lacked work. In all, he illustrated more than a hundred books in both black and white and watercolour.

Charles remained close to his brothers, Thomas and William, the second of whom gave the name 'Heath Robinson' a place in the English language. In later life the three of them founded a walking club in Pinner called 'The Frothfinders' Federation'.

FRANCES HODGSON BURNETT *The Secret Garden*
Illustrated by Charles Robinson

Little Lord Fauntleroy
Illustrated by C. E. Brock

LEWIS CARROLL *Alice's Adventures in Wonderland
and Through the Looking Glass*
Illustrated by John Tenniel

MIGUEL DE CERVANTES *Don Quixote of the Mancha*
Illustrated by Walter Crane

ROALD DAHL *The BFG*
Illustrated by Quentin Blake

DANIEL DEFOE *Robinson Crusoe*
Illustrated by W. J. Linton and others

CHARLES DICKENS *A Christmas Carol*
Illustrated by Arthur Rackham

SIR ARTHUR CONAN DOYLE *Sherlock Holmes*
Illustrated by Sidney Paget

RICHARD DOYLE *Jack the Giant Killer*
Illustrated by Richard Doyle

ALEXANDRE DUMAS *The Three Musketeers*
Illustrated by Edouard Zier

C. S. EVANS *Cinderella*
Illustrated by Arthur Rackham

The Sleeping Beauty
Illustrated by Arthur Rackham

OLIVER GOLDSMITH, WILLIAM COWPER and OTHERS
*Ride a-Cock-Horse and other
Rhymes and Stories*
Illustrated by Randolph Caldecott

KENNETH GRAHAME *The Wind in the Willows*
Illustrated by Arthur Rackham

ROGER LANCELYN GREEN *The Adventures of Robin Hood*
Illustrated by Walter Crane

King Arthur and his Knights
of the Round Table
Illustrated by Aubrey Beardsley

THE BROTHERS GRIMM *Fairy Tales*
Illustrated by Arthur Rackham

NATHANIEL HAWTHORNE *A Wonder-Book for Girls and Boys*
Illustrated by Arthur Rackham

JOSEPH JACOBS *English Fairy Tales*
Illustrated by John Batten

WALTER JERROLD *Mother Goose's Nursery Rhymes*
Illustrated by Charles Robinson

RUDYARD KIPLING *The Jungle Book*
Illustrated by Kurt Wiese

Just So Stories
Illustrated by the Author

JEAN DE LA FONTAINE *Fables*
Illustrated by R. de la Nézière

EDWARD LEAR *A Book of Nonsense*
Illustrated by the Author

GEORGE MACDONALD *At the Back of the North Wind*
Illustrated by Arthur Hughes

The Princess and the Goblin
Illustrated by Arthur Hughes

L. M. MONTGOMERY *Anne of Green Gables*
Illustrated by Sybil Tawse

E. NESBIT *The Railway Children*
Illustrated by C. E. Brock

BARONESS ORCZY *The Scarlet Pimpernel*